比较文学与世界文学 研究丛书

主编 曹顺庆

三编 第 **24** 册

出自一本书的 180 个成语(下)

吴 国 珍 编译

花木兰文化事业有限公司

国家图书馆出版品预行编目资料

出自一本书的 180 个成语（下）／吴国珍 编译 —— 初版 —— 新
北市：花木兰文化事业有限公司，2024〔民 113 〕
目 6+178 面；19×26 公分
（比较文学与世界文学研究丛书 三编 第 24 册）
ISBN 978-626-344-823-0（精装）
1.CST：论语 2.CST：成语 3.CST：注释 4.CST：白话译文
810.8   113009377

ISBN-978-626-344-823-0

9 786263 448230

比较文学与世界文学研究丛书
三编 第二四册   ISBN：978-626-344-823-0

出自一本书的 180 个成语（下）

编　译 吴国珍
主　编 曹顺庆
企　划 四川大学双一流学科暨比较文学研究基地
总 编 辑 杜洁祥
副总编辑 杨嘉乐
编辑主任 许郁翎
编　辑 潘玟静、蔡正宣　美术编辑 陈逸婷
出　版 花木兰文化事业有限公司
发 行 人 高小娟
联络地址 台湾 235 新北市中和区中安街七二号十三楼
　　　　 电话：02-2923-1455 ／传真：02-2923-1452
网　址 http://www.huamulan.tw 信箱 service@huamulans.com
印　刷 普罗文化出版广告事业
初　版 2024 年 9 月
定　价 三编 26 册（精装）新台币 70,000 元

出自一本书的 180 个成语(下)

吴国珍 编译

目次

下　册

091 匹夫之谅

to show minor fidelity like a common person
an ordinary person's minor fidelity
像普通人那样为小节而尽忠
一个普通人信守的小节

【出处】

子曰："微管仲，吾其被发左衽矣。岂若匹夫匹妇之为谅也，自经于沟渎而莫之知也。"（论语 14.17）

The Master said, "But for Guan Zhong, we might now be wearing our hair unbound with barbarian clothes on.

"How can you expect him to show minor fidelity (to his late master) like a common man or woman, and hang himself in a small valley without being known to any?"

Note: Guan Zhong's original master was killed by Prince Huan of the State of Qi, but he turned to Prince Huan to serve him. People said that he had no moral integrity. But Guan Zhong helped Prince Huan to reduce internal wars, repel foreign invasions and ensure 40 years of peace in the Kingdom of Zhou. Confucius said that this reflected Guan Zhon's moral integrity, and that if he had committed suicide to repay his original master as ordinary people did, it would not be a worthy death.

【今译】

孔子说："如果没有管仲，恐怕我们也要披散着头发，衣襟向左开了。哪能要求他像普通百姓那样信守小节（为他已故的主人殉节），在小山沟里上吊自杀而不能为世所知呀。"

【注释】

1. 谅：遵守信用，这里指坚守小节小信。
2. 自经：上吊自杀。

【解读】

　　管仲的故主为齐桓公所杀，但他转投桓公并为他服务。有人说他没有道德操守。但是，管仲辅助桓公减少内部争战，击退外来入侵，为周王国确保 40 年的和平。孔子说，这反映了管仲的节操，如果他像普通人一样为故主殉身效忠，那就死得不值。

【句例】

　　1. 他那种匹夫之谅对国家实在无益。

He *showed only minor fidelity like a common person*. That was not a help to the country.

　　2. 大人物要成大事就不能有匹夫之谅。

A great personage should not have *an ordinary person's minor fidelity* as he is to accomplish something great.

092 千乘之国

a state which has a thousand chariots
a powerful state
一个拥有一千辆兵车的国家；
一个强国

【出处】

子曰："道千乘之国，敬事而言，节用而爱人，使民以时。（论语 1.5）

The Master said, "To rule a state which has a thousand chariots, the ruler should devote himself to government affairs and keep his promise; he should retrench expenditure and cherish his subordinates; he should employ labor force only at proper time."

Note: Confucius told a state ruler about how to behave rightly so as to govern the state well. It also reflected Confucius' people-oriented thought as he encouraged the ruler to love his subordinates and the common people, and tried to dissuade him from requisitioning labor force randomly.

【今译】

孔子说："治理一个拥有千辆兵车的国家，要严谨认真地处理国家大事而又恪守诺言，节约财政开支而又爱护下属，征用民力要适得其时。"

【注释】

1. 道：同"导"。领导，治理。

2. 千乘之国：古代指兵力强大的国家。"乘"为四匹马拉的战车，借指它所配备的兵力。

【解读】

本句讲孔子为国君指出的治国原则和施政建议。把国君自身的修养和他对下属（人）和百姓（民）的关爱作为施政成功的保证，体现了早期儒家的民本思想。

【句例】

1. 千乘之国的国君，往往要受百乘之家家主的控制，这是春秋时期常有的事。

A ruler of *a state which had a thousand chariots* used to be controlled by a chief of a fiefdom with one hundred chariots. That was a common occurrence during the Spring and Autumn Period.

2. 要成为一个千乘之国，就要国土广、人口多，但关键还要有正确的治国理念。

It needs vast land and large population to make *a powerful state*, but the key is to have the correct ideas of governance.

093　巧言令色

artful words and flattering countenance
clever talks and ingratiating looks
花言巧语，装出一副讨好的嘴脸

【出处】

子曰："巧言令色，鲜矣仁。"（论语 1.3）

The Master said, "Artful words and flattering countenance have little to do with human goodness."

Note: Confucius pointed out that a man of rhetoric and flattery often lacked virtue, and it was essential to view a person by looking into his nature instead of his sweet words and flattery face.

【今译】

孔子说："花言巧语，装出一副讨好的嘴脸，（这种人的）仁德就很少了。"

【注释】

1. 巧言令色：花言巧语和讨好的面色。

【解读】

孔子指出，惯用甜言蜜语和阿谀奉承的人往往缺乏仁德，因此，看人要看本质，而不受其甜言蜜语和谄媚的脸色所蒙蔽。

【句例】

1. 新来的秘书极尽巧言令色之能事，人人看了都恶心。

The new secretary resorts to all sorts of *artful words and flattering countenance*, which disgusts everybody.

2. 他的巧言令色忽悠过了几乎所有的人，唯独我们的总经理助理从来不买他的账。

His *clever talks and ingratiating looks* have fooled almost everyone except our assistant general manager who would never buy it.

094 切问近思

to ask questions of immediate concern and
ponder over things closely around;
to inquire and think about relevant questions
提出切身的问题，思考身边的事物
提出并思考密切相关的问题

【出处】

子夏曰："博学而笃志，切问而近思，仁在其中矣。"（论语 19.6）

Zixia said, "Broaden your learning and firmly remember what is learned, ask questions of immediate concern and ponder over things closely around, and you are on the way to moral perfection."

Note: Zixia believed that it was not difficult to reach the realm of benevolence. He thought that apart from learning extensively, a person should also be good at thinking. He was opposed to thinking about some big and impractical problems, and thought it necessary to focus on things closely related to reality, and think about solutions to the problems.

【今译】

子夏说："博览群书，扩展学问，牢牢记住所学过的东西，提出切身的问题，思考身边的事物，仁就在其中了。"

【注释】

1. 切问：提出紧密相关的问题；提出切合实际情况的问题。

【解读】

子夏认为要达到仁的境界并不难。他认为除了广泛学习之外，还要善于思考问题。他反对思考一些虚无缥缈的、大而无当的问题，而提倡要专注于与现实生活密切相关的事情，从中思考解决问题的方法。

【句例】

1. 这个计划关系到普通民众的日常生活，制定时宜先切问近思，切忌好高骛远。

This plan is related to the daily life of the ordinary people, so when making it we should first *ask questions of immediate concern and ponder over things closely around*, and try not to be overly ambitious.

2. 他切问近思，所提方案都符合国家的实际情况。

He *inquired and thought about relevant questions*, so all the proposals he put forward were in line with the actual situation of the country.

095　求仁得仁

to sacrifice for what one pursues
to sacrifice for a just cause
As you brew, so you must drink. (ironical)
为实现自己的追求而献
身为正义事业而牺牲
自作自受（讽刺性用法）

【出处】

冉有曰："伯夷、叔齐何人也？"曰："古之贤人也。"曰："怨乎？"曰："求仁而得仁，又何怨。"（论语 7.15）

Zigong asked, "What sort of men were Boyi and Shuqi , Sir?"

"Ancient virtuous people," said the Master.

"Were they regretful for what they had done?" Zigong asked again.

"They sacrificed for what they had pursued. So why regretful?"

Note: When Confucius was in the State of Wei, some of his disciples were also there working for Prince Chu, the new state ruler. They assumed that Confucius would also support Prince Chu because his father Kuai Kui was exiled after failure in a plan to kill his mother who he believed had usurped the state power. However, Confucius quoted the story of Boyi and Shuqi who tried hard to give up the throne to each other. He implied that the son should give up the throne to the father as filial piety should always come first. This showed that Confucius did not support Prince Chu.

【今译】

冉有问孔子："伯夷、叔齐是什么样的人呢？"（孔子）说："古代的贤人。"（冉有又）问："他们后悔了吗？"（孔子）说："他们求仁而得到了仁，为什么会后悔呢？"

【注释】

1. 伯夷、叔齐：古代著名隐士。

2. 求仁而得仁，又何怨：现指为追求正义事业而献身，死而无怨。

【解读】

　　当时子路等人正在为卫出公服务，而卫出公跟他的父亲正在争位。孔子在子贡的面前赞扬伯夷和叔齐两位隐士，实际上是在赞扬他们的让国精神。伯夷、叔齐是商末孤竹君的两个儿子。相传其父遗命要立叔齐为继承人。孤竹君死后，叔齐要大哥伯夷继位，伯夷不受，因为他必须遵从父命。叔齐也不愿继位，因为他必须尊重兄长。二人先后逃往周国，最后饿死在首阳山下。孔子说这两兄弟是为了追求孝和悌而作出牺牲，所以他们虽死无悔。孔子赞扬伯夷和叔齐，等于暗示卫出公应该让位给他的父亲，这是孝道的要求。子贡听了孔子的话，回去对子路说，我们老师不支持卫出公呀。子路不听，继续支持卫出公，结果在宫廷内斗中被杀身亡。

【句例】

　　1. 英雄们求仁得仁，死得其所。

The heroes *sacrificed for the just cause* and theirs was a worthy death.

　　2. 那是他自己要的。求仁得仁，没什么可后悔的。

That's what he chose for himself. *As he brewed, so he must drink*. There is nothing to repent.

096　犬马之养

even dogs and horses may also get fed
to support parents like feeding animals (a wrong doing!)
狗和马尚且能得到饲养
供养父母如同饲养牲口（错误的做法！）

【出处】

子游问孝，子曰："今之孝者，是谓能养。至于犬马，皆能有养，不敬，何以别乎？"（论语 2.7）

When Ziyou asked how to show filial piety, the Master said, "Nowadays filial piety simply means the feeding of one's parents. But since dogs and horses may also get fed, what is there to distinguish the two (kinds of "feeding") if one shows no respect while supporting the parents?"

Note: Confucius told his disciple Ziyou (named YanYan) that it was not enough only to support the parents materially, and a respectful attitude toward them was of first importance.

【今译】

子游问什么是孝，孔子说："如今所谓的孝，只是说能给父母饭吃就够了。然而，既然连犬马都能够得到饲养，那么如果不心存敬意，赡养父母与饲养犬马又有什么区别呢？"

【注释】

1. 养：（对人）赡养；（对动物）饲养。

【解读】

孔子指出，孝敬父母不能光考虑从物质上满足他们，还要让他们感觉到精神上的愉悦，这是儒家孝道最为人性化的一面，但也是子女最容易忽视的一点。

【句例】

1. 犬马之养尚且人人皆知，赡养父母岂能不带敬意？

Everyone knows that *even dogs and horses may get fed*, so how can we support our parents without respect?

2. 他对父母作犬马之养，真不是人！

He supported his parents like feeding animals. He could not be counted as a human !

097　群而不党　矜而不争

to be sociable, but do not gang up
to be sociable but not clannish
to be dignified, but do not contend against each other
合群而不结党营私
合群而不排外
庄重而与人无争

【出处】

子曰："君子矜而不争，群而不党。"（论语 15.22）

The Master said, "Men of virtue are dignified, but do not contend against each other. They are sociable, but do not gang up."

Note: Confucius pointed out that men of virtue should not contend against each other or form small cliques.

【今译】

孔子说："君子庄重而与人无争，合群而不结党营私。"

【注释】

1. 党：结派。

2. 矜：庄重。

【解读】

此句讲君子的待人处世之道。君子在这里当指品德高尚的人，他们往往显得矜持而脸色庄重，给人凛然不可侵犯的感觉，但其实，他们只是固守原则，却不作无谓的争论，更不会争吵。他们广为团结而不拉帮结派，体现出正直无私的优秀品质。这原则同样适用于有位者的君子。一个领导人做到这一点，就能维护自己的尊严和威望，团结大多数把工作做好。

【句例】

1. 这几位文人专心做学问，群而不党。

These men of letters concentrate on academic studies. They are *sociable but not clannish.*

2. 高情商的人明白事理，矜而不争。

People with high EQ (emotional quotient) are rational; they are *dignified but will not contend against each other.*

098 人而无信，不知其可

It isn't all right for a man to go without credibility.
A man cannot go without credibility.
一个人不可以不讲信用。

【出处】

子曰："人而无信，不知其可也。大车无輗，小车无軏，其何以行之哉？"
（论语 2.22）

The Master said, "I don't think it all right for a man to go without credibility.
How can a large carriage or a small one be made to go without the crossbar?"

Note: Confucius emphasized the importance of good credibility. According to him, credibility
to a man was just like a crossbar to a carriage, and a man without credibility was like a
carriage without its crossbar and could hardly go a step forward.

【今译】

孔子说："一个人没有信用是不可以的。就好像大车没有輗、小车没有軏
一样，它靠什么行走呢？"

【注释】

1. 輗：古代车辕前面横木上的木销子，用于大车。
2. 軏：古代车辕前面横木上的木销子，用于小车。

【解读】

孔子以行车作比喻强调诚信缺失的严重后果，他认为，一个人就像一驾马
车，而信誉就像马车横木上的木销子，看起来不明显，却是一个关键部件，没
了它，马车就会散架，无法向前迈进一步。

【句例】

1. 人而无信，不知其可，所以希望你能按时还债。
It isn't all right for a man to go without credibility, so it is hoped that you will

pay the debts on time.

2. 人而无信，不知其可，这个道理人人明白，却有不少人每天都在违犯它。

A man cannot go without credibility. Everyone knows about this reason but there are quite a lot of people who violate it every day.

099 人无远虑，必有近忧

Those who have no long-term worries are
bound to have some short-term ones.
One cannot but meet with troubles, either
long-term ones or immediate ones.
一个人即使没有长远的忧虑，也难免会有某种眼前的忧虑。
人必有忧虑，不管是长远的还是眼前的。

【出处】

子曰："人无远虑，必有近忧。"（论语 15.12）

The Master said, "Those who have no long-term worries are bound to have some short-term ones."

Note: According to Confucius, life is full of ups and downs, and there will be hardships and worries that accompany a person all the time, either at present or in the future. Here Confucius was trying to warn people that everyone should be conscious of that and be prepared for any trouble or worries they might encounter at any stage of life.

【今译】

孔子说："一个人即使没有长远的忧虑，也难免会有某种眼前的忧虑。"

【注释】

1. 远虑、近忧：长远的忧虑和近在眼前的忧虑。

【解读】

此句告诫人们要常常心怀忧患意识。人生在世，忧患是常态，没有大的，也会有小的；没有长远的，也会有短期的。此句多本有不同解读，其一是：如果一个人没有长远的考虑，就必然会招致眼前的忧患。此说逻辑不通。"没有长远的考虑"是"因"，它的"果"必然是出在将来，不可能出在现在。

【句例】

1. 人无远虑，必有近忧。谁敢说他永远不会碰到困难和挫折？

Those who have no long-term worries are bound to have some short-term ones. Who dare say he will never encounter difficulties and setbacks?

2. 人无远虑，必有近忧，我们要常怀忧患意识，保持冷静的头脑。

A man cannot but meet with troubles, either long-term ones or immediate ones, so we should always be crisis-conscious and calm-headed.

100　人之将死，其言也善
鸟之将死，其鸣也哀

When a man is dying, he utters kind remarks.
When a bird is dying, it makes mournful cries.
一个人快死的时候，说的话是善意的。
鸟快死的时候，叫声是悲哀的。

【出处】

曾子有疾，孟敬子问之。曾子言曰："鸟之将死，其鸣也哀；人之将死，其言也善。"（论语 8.4）

Zengzi was very ill and Mengjingzi went to see him. Zengzi said, "When a bird is dying, it makes mournful cries; when a man is dying, he utters kind remarks."

Note: Mengjingzi was a high-ranking official of the State of Lu. When he came to visit Zengzi who was dying, Zengzi listed some of his shortcomings hoping that he would correct them. Zengzi used to be Mengjingzi's opponent. To make his "enemy" believe him, he began his advice with that old saying, as if to say, "I am dying, and a dying man will not lie, so please believe me."

【今译】

曾子有病，孟敬子去看望他。曾子对他说："鸟快死的时候，叫声是悲哀的；人快死的时候，说的话是善意的。"

【注释】

1. 孟敬子：鲁国大夫孟孙捷。

【解读】

曾子临死前孟敬子来探望他。曾子跟孟敬子有过对立，临死前想针对他平时的缺点给他提出几条忠告，故讲这话时特意引用"鸟之将死，其鸣也哀"的古话，意思是，一个临死的人不会说谎的，希望对方相信自己的真诚。曾子在生命即将结束时还想着别人，而且是曾经与自己有过过结的人，其胸怀之宽广令人赞叹。

【句例】

1. 鸟之将死，其鸣也哀；人之将死，其言也善。你爷爷临终前给你指出的缺点，你一定要照改呀。

When a bird is dying, it makes mournful cries; when a man is dying, he utters kind remarks. You must correct the shortcomings that your grandpa pointed out to you when he was dying.

2. 或许是人之将死其言也善吧，这位死囚的话实在是发人深省。

It may be true that *a man who is dying will utter kind remarks*. What the prisoner said before he was executed sounded so sobering.

101　任重道远

to shoulder weighty responsibilities and have a long way ahead
a long-term and arduous task a long way to go
责任重大，奋斗的道路很长
长期而艰巨的任务有很长的路要走

【出处】

曾子曰："士不可以不弘毅，任重而道远。仁以为己任，不亦重乎？死而后已，不亦远乎？"（论语 8.7）

Zengzi said, "A scholar cannot but aim high and be perseverant, for he has to shoulder weighty responsibilities with a long way ahead. Isn't it weighty when he has to take it as his responsibility to help rule with benevolent governance? Isn't it long when he has to work all the way until his death? "

Note: Zengzi pointed out that a scholar should have a lofty ambition and great perseverance so as to shoulder great responsibilities in helping with state administration.

【今译】

曾子说："士不可不志向远大，意志坚强，因为他肩负着重大使命，道路又很漫长。以实行仁道为己任，这副担子还不重吗？要奋斗终身，到死才停止，这条道路还不漫长吗？"

【注释】

1. 士：当时的知识分子，一般是不能继承爵禄的贵族后代，后来也有少数平民子弟通过熟习礼乐知识而成为士的。这类人不治产业，只能以自己的学识、才能和忠诚为统治阶级服务。

2. 弘毅：志向宏大，品格刚毅。

【解读】

西周时期主要的治国辅助力量是君子，尤其是贵族出身的卿大夫。到了春秋晚期和战国初期，士作为治国的辅助力量已经崛起。孔子的不少学生就成了这样的士。曾子要求士要有强烈的正义感和社会责任感，要能在协助国君以德治国方面承担重任、奋斗终身。

【句例】

1. 在实现重建祖国的宏伟目标的道路上，我们任重道远。

We *shoulder weighty responsibilities and have a long way ahead* in achieving the grand goal of the reconstruction of our country.

2. 对于当时的政府来说，要在那么大的范围内扫除文盲应该是任重而道远。

For the government of that time, it should be *a long-term and arduous task* to eliminate illiteracy on such a large scale.

102　三人行，必有我师

In a party of three there must be one whom I can learn from.
You can always find a teacher even within a small crowd.
三人同行，肯定有一个是值得我学习的。
即使在一个不大的人群中，你也总是可以找到一位老师。

【出处】

子曰："三人行，必有我师焉。择其善者而从之，其不善者而改之。"（论语 7.22）

The Master said, "In a party of three there must be one whom I can learn from. I will pick his merits to emulate them, and find his demerits to amend mine."

Note: Confucius meant that even among a small number of people there ought to be one who was worth his learning from. It shows Confucius' eagerness and modesty in learning. Confucius didn't have a regular teacher and he did learn from many other people. Moreover, Confucius not only learned from those who had good qualities, but also drew lessons from others' wrongdoings so as to help correct his own, and that was where his wisdom lay.

【今译】

孔子说："三人同行，肯定有一个是值得我学习的。我选择他们的优点而加以仿效，并找出他们的缺点以改掉我身上类似的缺点。"

【注释】

1. 三人行：指为数不多的一群人，不是说三个人一起走路。

【解读】

"三人行"指为数不多的一群人。在极小的一群人中便有我可以师法的人，而四海之大，值得我学习的人就更多了。这是说一个人只要肯学习，则到处都有值得师法的人，可以做到学无常师。孔子本身就是学无常师的典范。孔子不但好学，而且善于学习，学无常法。他提倡以不善者为师，是要参照别人身上的不善而作自我检查，改掉自身类似的不善，这是一种高度自觉的学习。

【句例】

1. "三人行必有我师。"这次世博会是我们向世界各国学习的大好机会。

"*In a party of three there must be one whom I can learn from.*" This world expo offers us a wonderful opportunity to learn from other countries.

2. 古人说，三人行，必有我师。你到那里后要虚心向别人学习。

The ancients said that *you can always find a teacher even within a small crowd*, so when you get there you must learn modestly from others.

103 三省吾身

to ask oneself several times in daily introspection
to reflect on oneself several times a day
每日多次自我反省

【出处】

曾子曰：“吾日三省吾身。为人谋而不忠乎？与朋友交而不信乎？传不习乎？”（论语 7.22）

Zengzi said, "I ask myself several times in my daily introspection: Am I not dedicated when handling affairs for others? Am I not trustworthy to my friends? Have I not reviewed the lessons taught by the teacher?"

Note: Confucius' disciple Zengzi described how he reflected himself every day. Zeng Shen learnt diligently and kept self-cultivating and became a very good disciple of Confucius'. He was modest, cautious and strict with himself, and often thought of being good and helpful to others.

【今译】

曾子说：“我每天多次反省自己：为别人办事尽心尽力了吗？同朋友交往做到诚实可信了吗？老师传授的学业复习了吗？”

【注释】

1. 省：反省，自我检查。

【解读】

孔子的弟子曾子（曾参）描述了他每天如何反省自己。曾参勤奋学习，不断自我修养，成为孔子的优秀弟子。他谦虚谨慎，对自己要求严格，经常想着对别人好，帮助别人。

【句例】

1. 我每日三省吾身。工作任务完成了吗？创新研究有进展了吗？身体锻炼没有中断吗?

I *ask myself several times in my daily introspection*: Have I finished my work assignment? Is there any progress in my innovation research? Have I interrupted my physical exercise?

2. 我每日三省吾身,就是怕身上有什么缺点会给工作带来损失。

I *reflect on myself several times a day* for fear that my defects will bring losses to my work.

104　三十而立

to begin to stand firm on one's own feet at thirty
to stand on one's own feet in one's thirties
三十岁开始自立

【出处】

子曰："吾十有五而志于学，三十而立，四十而不惑，五十而知天命，六十而耳顺，七十而从心所欲不逾矩。"（论语 2.4）

The Master said, "At the age of fifteen I began to devote myself to learning; at thirty I began to stand firm on my own feet; in my forties I was free from puzzlement; when I turned fifty I had come to apperceive destiny; by the age of sixty I had been all ears to different opinions; now in my seventies I can follow what my heart desires without going against what is right."

Note: At the age of thirty, Confucius began to enter society and establish himself in society. At that time, he gradually became knowledgeable and recognized by society. At the same time, he began to have disciples and taught them classical knowledge and some important skills.

【今译】

孔子说："我十五岁立志于学习；三十岁开始能立足社会；四十岁能不被外界事物所迷惑；五十岁懂得了天命；六十岁能听取各种不同言论或意见；七十岁能随心所欲而不越出规矩。"

【注释】

1. 有：同"又"。
2. 立：指能自己立足于社会。

【解读】

三十岁时，孔子开始进入社会并在社会上立足。那时，他逐渐变得知识渊博并得到社会的认可。与此同时，他开始收徒，并向他们传授经典知识和一些重要技能。

【句例】

1. 到了三十而立的时候，我们应当好好思考自己的人生目标。

When we *begin to stand firm on our own feet at thirty*, we should have a good think of our goal of life.

2. 你儿子现在已经是三十而立了。你不要过分关心他。

Your son has *been able to stand on his own feet in his thirties*. You needn't care too much about him.

105　三思而后行

to think thrice before one acts
to look before one leaps (English idiom)
反复考虑后再去做。

【出处】

季文子三思而后行。子闻之，曰："再，斯可矣。"（论语 5.20）

Jiwenzi thought thrice before he acted. When the Master learned about that, he said, "Twice will do."

Note: "Thinking thrice before one acts" is certainly a good thing, but Confucius suggested that Jiwenzi should think only twice and that was enough. Isn't that strange? It turns out that Jiwenzi was famous for his caution, but since he was too cautious, he became timid and small-minded, so Confucius hoped that he would get rid of the shortcomings of being too cautious. This statement of Confucius should be seen as an isolated case rather than a general theory, because he had always advocated caution.

【今译】

季文子每做一件事都要考虑三次。孔子听到后说："两次就行了。"

【注释】

1. 季文子：即季孙行父，于鲁成公、鲁襄公时任正卿，"文"是他的谥号。

2. 再：两次。

【解读】

"三思而后行"本来是件好事，但孔子却建议季文子"两思"就够了。这不是很奇怪吗？原来，季文子以谨慎出名，但谨慎过了头，就变得畏缩和小器，故孔子希望他改掉过分谨慎的缺点。孔子此言应看作仅针对个例，并非普适之论，因为他一惯提倡谨言慎行。

【句例】

1. 这个计划的实施对公司的兴衰关系重大，你们得三思而后行。

The implementation of this plan matters much to the rise or fall of the company.

You should *think thrice before you act*.

2. 李先生以前总是三思而后行，所以他很少出错。

Mr. Li used to *look before he leapt*, so he seldom erred.

106 三月不知肉味

to feel meat tasteless for three months (to be absorbed
in something only to forget about other fun);
to have no meat for meals for a long time (a variant)
有三个月的时间尝不出肉的美味
很长时间没吃到肉（后世变体）

【出处】

子在齐闻《韶》，三月不知肉味，曰："不图为乐之至于斯也。"（论语 7.14）

Enjoying the music *Shao* in the State of Qi, the Master felt meat tasteless for three months, and said, "Never expected that music playing could be charming to that extent."

Note: Confucius was so fascinated with the music *Shao* that he even forgot the taste of his favorite food. When Confucius was 35, his state ruler was forced to go into exile in the State of Qi. He also went to Qi, where he discussed music with the grand musician, heard the music *Shao* and learnt it, and loved it so dearly.

【今译】

孔子在齐国听到了《韶》乐，竟然有三个月的时间尝不出肉的美味，他说，"想不到音乐的演奏竟然达到了这样迷人的地步。"

【注释】

1.《韶》：相传是古代歌颂舜的一种乐舞。

2. 三月不知肉味：三个月之内吃肉不觉得有味道。比喻沉浸于某一乐趣而忘了其他乐趣。后世也借指长时间没吃到肉。

【解读】

孔子 35 岁时到了齐国。这期间他与齐国太师论乐，听了《韶》乐后，一直陶醉在其优美的旋律中，以至于淡忘了别的生活乐趣。这首先是因为他精通乐理懂得欣赏，其次是他对《韶》乐的尊崇。《韶》相传是歌颂舜的一种乐舞，反映的是尧禅让于舜的一种政权的"和平过渡"。身居乱世看到太多争战杀伐的孔子，对那个"理想社会"当然无比向往。爱屋及乌，孔子对这乐舞自然赞美有加。

【句例】

1. 听完他的大提琴独奏会，很多人说回家后他们三月不知肉味。

Having attended his cello recital, many people said that when they were back at home they *felt meat tasteless for three months.*

2. 当年的物质生活极端贫乏，连富贵人家也常常是三月不知肉味。

In those years when the material life was extremely poor, even the rich people *had no meat for meals for a long time.*

107 色厉内荏

to appear severe outwardly but is timid inwardly
an ass in a lion's skin
外表严厉而内心虚弱
外强中干

【出处】

子曰："色厉而内荏，譬诸小人，其犹穿窬之盗也与?"（论语 17.12）

The Master said, "He who appears severe outwardly but is timid inwardly may be compared to a base man, or perhaps a thief who pierces through or climbs over a wall."

Note: Confucius denounced some people who made a stern appearance in order to conceal their inner weakness and timidity, and said they were like thieves who were stealing.

【今译】

孔子说："外表严厉而内心虚弱，以小人作比喻，大概就像挖墙洞的窃贼吧?"

【注释】

1. 色厉内荏：外表严厉而内心虚弱。厉，威严；荏，虚弱。

2. 窬：洞。

【解读】

孔子谴责一些人企图以外表的严厉来掩饰内心的怯懦，说他们就像行窃的小偷一样。

【句例】

1. 他们屡屡对我们发起挑战，那是色厉内荏的表现。他们惯用虚张声势来掩盖内心的恐惧。

They have launched a series of challenge to us. It shows that they *appear severe outwardly but are timid inwardly*. They have been resorting to bravado to hide their fears.

2. 我们情不自禁地嘲笑他，因为大家都知道他只是个色厉内荏的胆小鬼。

We could not but laugh at him since we all know that he is *an ass in a lion's skin*.

108　杀身成仁

to give up one's life for a just cause
to sacrifice oneself to keep to moral integrity
为正义事业而献出生命
牺牲性命以保全仁德

【出处】

子曰："志士仁人，无求生以害仁，有杀身以成仁。"（论语 15.9）

The Master said, "A man of ideal and moral integrity should not seek to survive at the expense of morality, but should be ready to give up his life for a just cause."

Note: Confucius pointed out that one should dare to sacrifice his life for justice at the critical moment and should not seek to survive by immoral means.

【今译】

孔子说："志士仁人，不能牺牲仁德来保全性命，而是要牺牲性命来保全仁德。"

【注释】

1. 志士仁人：指有高尚志向和道德情操的人。
2. 害仁：损害仁德，违背道德价值。
3. 杀身以成仁：为维护道德和正义而献身。

【解读】

孔子指出为人要有献身理想的愿望和勇气。人的生命是可贵的，但孔子认为在关键时刻，一个人不能以牺牲道德价值为代价来苟全性命，而要能为维护道德和正义而献身。

【句例】

1. 他们杀身以成仁的英雄气概鼓舞了无数的后来人。

They *gave their lives for the just cause*, and their heroic spirit has been inspiring countless followers.

2. 弹尽粮绝之际，所有守城战士们宁愿杀身成仁也不向敌人投降。

Having used up all their ammunition and food, all the soldiers who guarded the city would rather *sacrifice themselves to keep to moral integrity* than surrender to the enemy.

109　上智下愚

the wise of the highest class and the stupid of the lowest class
上等的智者与下等的愚者

【出处】

子曰："唯上知与下愚不移。"（论语 17.3）

The Master said, "Only the wise of the highest class and the stupid of the lowest class are not to be changed."

Note: Confucius pointed out that it was hard for those who were extremely clever and extremely stupid to change their intelligence states. He seemed to mean that education should be given to the so-called "average people", or people who were not too clever and not too stupid.

【今译】

孔子说："只有上等的智者与下等的愚者是改变不了的。"

【注释】

1. 上知：有上等智慧的人。知，同"智"。

2. 下愚：最低一级的愚者，最愚蠢的人。

3. 不移：不会改变，意即即使给予后天的教育也难以改变。

【解读】

关于"上知与下愚不移"历来解读不同，主要有三种：一、孔子认为统治阶级聪明而被统治阶级愚蠢。但孔子弟子几乎都来自被统治阶级，而孔子孜孜以求的，正是通过教育改变他们，所以这个说法不通。二、"上智"是地位高贵而又聪明的人，"下愚"是地位低下而又愚蠢的人，前者有机会接受良好教育，不至于变坏；后者没有机会接受教育，故难以提升，其智愚难以改变。持此说者认为孔子是在客观地指出这一社会现状，本书采纳这一解读。三、上智是生而知之者，下愚是困而不学者，前者不容易变坏，后者难以变好，唯不上不下的"中人"，可善可恶，正是这类人须要加以教育，此说也有一定的道理。

【句例】

1. 既然他认为上智下愚不可改变，他就集中精力教育所谓的"中人"。

Since he believed that *the wise of the highest class and the stupid of the lowest class* were not to be changed, he focused on the education of the so-called "average people".

2. 哟，你们是上智，我们是下愚，改不了啦！最好各走各的路。

Well, well, you are *the wise of the highest class and we are the stupid of the lowest class, and cannot be changed*! Better go on our own ways.

110　深厉浅揭

A deep river must be crossed with the clothes on; a shallow river may be crossed with the clothes lifted up.
to deal with different situations flexibly
水深就穿着衣服趟过去，水浅就撩起衣服趟过去。
按不同情况灵活处事

【出处】

子击磬于卫，有荷蒉而过孔氏之门者，曰："有心哉，击磬乎！"既而曰："鄙哉！硁硁乎！莫己知也，斯己而已矣。深则厉，浅则揭。"（论语 14.39）

Once while he was in the State of Wei, Confucius was playing the chime stone in a house when a man with a straw basket on his back came passing by and said, "He is playing the chime stone with something at heart."

After a while he made another comment, saying, "How contemptible! It sounds shallow and stubborn, as if complaining about not being understood by others. If so, forget it then."

Then he added, "A deep river must be crossed with the clothes on; a shallow river may be crossed with the clothes lifted up."

Note: Confucius often felt sorry for his doctrine not being used. Now he admitted that his music playing did reveal the hidden sadness in his heart. The passer-by was a hermit. His last sentence above meant that Confucius should adapt to the situation and choose to live in reclusion.

【今译】

孔子在卫国，一次正在击磬奏乐，有一位背扛草筐的人从门前走过说："这个击磬的人有心事啊！"一会儿又说："声音浅薄而固执，真可鄙呀，像是在表明没有人了解自己，既然如此那就算了吧。（人生好像涉水一样）水深就穿着衣服趟过去，水浅就撩起衣服趟过去。"

【注释】

1. 硁硁：象声词，此处比喻人的顽固。

2. 深则厉：如果水深就穿着衣服涉水过河。

3. 浅则揭：如果水浅就提起衣襟涉水过河。

【解读】

此段反映另一位隐士对孔子的讽劝。这位隐士对音乐有很高的造诣，他从孔子击磬声中听出他的学说不为时所用、理想无法实现的心事，也听出他"知其不可而为之"的"顽固"心结。他隐讽孔子要顺应形势，干不了就不要硬干，就像过河那样，水深水浅要有不同的应对办法。他的意思是说孔子最好像他那样退而当个隐士。

【句例】

1. 古人的"深厉浅揭"，是说处理事情要灵活变通。

When the ancients said "*A deep river must be crossed with the clothes on; a shallow river may be crossed with the clothes lifted up*", they meant that one should be flexible in dealing with things.

2. 遇到难事要学会深厉浅揭，不可一味蛮干。

You should learn *to deal with difficulties flexibly*, and never do things blindly and foolishly.

111 慎终追远

Prudently perform funeral rites to the parents and
permanently remember the forefathers;
to observe funeral rites prudently and
always remember the ancestors
谨慎地料理父母的丧事，永远怀念自己的祖先
谨守丧礼，永志先人

【出处】

曾子曰："慎终追远，民德归厚矣。"（论语 1.9）

Zengzi said, "Prudently perform funeral rites to parents and permanently
remember forefathers, and the civic morality will resume its excellence."

Note: Zengzi held that taking last care of deceased kinsfolk and showing reverence to
forefathers would help resume pure folkways. He understood well that such practice was the
continuance of filial piety and filial piety was the foundation of moral excellence.

【今译】

曾子说："谨慎地料理父母的丧事，不忘怀念祭祀自己的祖先，民风就会
趋于淳厚。"

【注释】

1. 慎终：慎重处理父母的丧事。终，即寿终，这里指父母去世。
2. 追远：怀念祖先，按礼的要求祭祀祖先。远，即远祖、祖先。

【解读】

尊重先人是孝悌的延续，而孝悌是仁之本，曾子此说完全秉承孔子提倡的
孝道。孝道的体现，一是对父母等长辈在世时的物质和精神赡养，二是他们去
世后的殡葬和祭祀。做到这些，就是对亲人的爱，也是"仁"这一大爱的发端。
有了仁爱，民风自然就会淳朴敦厚。

【句例】

1. 按儒家的说法，慎终追远是孝道的延续。

According to Confucians, *to prudently perform funeral rites to parents and permanently remember forefathers* is the continuance of filial piety.

2. 这个民族有一种慎终追远的传统习俗。

This nation has a traditional custom of *observing funeral rites prudently and always remembering the ancestors*.

112　生而知之

to be born learned
to be born with knowledge
生来就有知识

【出处】

子曰："我非生而知之者，好古，敏以求之者也。"（论语 7.20）

The Master said, "I was not born learned. I simply love ancient things and diligently seek knowledge from them."

Note: Confucius didn't agree that he was born with knowledge, and said that he was interested in learning ancient culture and diligent in learning.

【今译】

孔子说："我不是生来就有知识的人，而是爱好古代的东西，并且勤奋地从中求取知识。"

【注释】

1. 敏：勤勉，敏捷。

【解读】

孔子不同意别人说他生而博学，而是说他对学习古代文化很感兴趣，也很勤奋。

【句例】

1. 在这个世界上，真正生而知之的人是没有的。

There is no one in the world who is truly *born learned*.

2. 你们可能以为孔子是生而知之的圣人。实际上，孔子说了，他小时候卑贱，所以学到了很多低微的技艺。

You people may think that Confucius was a sage *born with knowledge*. But the fact is, just as Confucius put it, that he was humble when young, so he learned a lot of menial skills.

113　生荣死哀

to live a glorious life, and die a mournful death
to enjoy great reverence whether living or dead
活着受人尊敬，死了使人哀痛
无论活着或死去都备受崇敬

【出处】

子贡曰："夫子之得邦家者，所谓立之斯立，道之斯行，绥之斯来，动之斯和。其生也荣，其死也哀，如之何其可及也？"（论语 19.25）

Zigong said, "Had my master been given a state or a feoff to govern, I should say he could have helped the people to stand on their own feet, led the people and caused them to follow, appeased the people to win them over, and gained their keen responses when he motivated them. "My master lived a glorious life, and died a mournful death. How could anyone be his equal?"

Note: When a fellow disciple asserted that Zigong was better than his teacher, Zigong sternly rejected the compliments. He had full confidence of the great talents of Confucius, and implied that it would be unwise to devalue Confucius. He believed that Confucius would enjoy great reverence whether he was living or dead.

【今译】

子贡说："老师他如果能获得治理诸侯国或封邑的权位，那就会像人们说的那样，要让他的人民有所建树，人民就能有所建树；要引导百姓，百姓就会跟着行动；要安抚百姓，百姓就会前来归附；要动员百姓，百姓就会齐心协力地应和。老师活着是十分荣耀的，死了极尽哀荣。有谁能赶得上他呢？"

【注释】

1. 绥之斯来：要安抚百姓，百姓就会前来归附。绥，安抚。
2. 动之斯和：要动员百姓，百姓就会齐心协力。和，协力。

【解读】

当一个同门弟子断言子贡比他的老师更好时，子贡严厉地拒绝了这些赞美。他对孔子的伟大才华充满信心，并暗示贬低孔子是不明智的。他相信孔子无论活着还是死去都会受到人们的崇敬。

【句例】

1. 岳飞是一位生荣死哀的民族英雄。

Yue Fei is a national hero who *lived a glorious life and died a mournful death.*

2. 为国为民鞠躬尽瘁，生荣死哀，这是他一生的写照。

This is the portrayal of his life: devoting all his life to serving the country and people, and *enjoying great reverence whether he was living or dead.*

114 升堂入室

to ascend to the hall and enter the chamber
to be raised from fairly good to highly proficient
to be highly proficient
由浅入深，逐步达到高深的造诣
高度娴熟

【出处】

子曰："由之瑟奚为于丘之门？"门人不敬子路。子曰．"由也升堂矣，未入于室也。"（论语 11.15）

The Master said, "Why must Zhong You play the zither at the door of my house?" What he said soon caused the other disciples to show no more respect for Zilu.

"But," added the Master, "Zhong You has ascended to the hall, except that he has not yet entered the chamber."

Note: Confucius made a negative response to Zilu's zither playing. When he realized that he had caused other disciples to disrespect Zilu, he made some more comments to affirm Zilu's progress, saying that he was playing fairly well (had ascended to the hall), though not quite perfectly (not yet entered the chamber), hoping that the other disciples would not disrespect him any longer.

【今译】

孔子说："仲由为什么跑到我这里来弹瑟呢？"孔子的学生们因此都不再尊敬子路。孔子便说："仲由嘛，已经达到升堂的程度了，只是还没有入室罢了。"

【注释】

1. 由：仲由，字子路，孔子的重要弟子。

2. 升堂入室：古时借三事比喻学问或技艺掌握程度的深浅：入门，即开始掌握最基本的知识或技艺；升堂，达到较高的程度；入室，达到娴熟高深的造诣。

【解读】

孔子先批评子路弹瑟弹得不好，后来看到其他弟子因此而轻视子路，便又对子路略加肯定，说他虽未"入室"，亦已"升堂"，意思是说子路虽然还达不到娴熟高深的造诣，但已经达到较高的程度了，希望能以此挽回影响。

【句例】

1. 古人用升堂入室来比喻某人的学问或技能的程度。升堂表示较好，入室表示达到最高专业水准。

The ancients used "*ascending to the hall and entering the chamber*" to describe one's knowledge or skill level. "Ascending to the hall" means being fairly good; "entering the chamber" means being highly proficient.

2. 经过大量艰苦的训练，她的钢琴演奏技巧可以说是升堂入室了。

After receiving a great amount of arduous training, she can be said to *be highly proficient* in piano playing.

115　食不厌精，脍不厌细

do not indulge in refined cereal or delicious meat
do not indulge in delicious food
never reject a delicious cuisine (a misreading)
不过分享用精细美味的粮米和鱼肉
不过分享用美食
美食不嫌其精细（一种误读）

【出处】

食不厌精，脍不厌细。（论语 10.8）

(The Master) did not indulge in refined cereal or delicious meat.

Note: This is the first sentence of a long passage that reveals how Confucius observed some good dining habits and some taboos. Confucius' dietary taboo was that he would not consume too much delicious food.

【今译】

（孔子）不会过分享用精细美味的粮米和鱼肉。

【注释】

1. 食不厌精，脍不厌细：此句向来有两种解读。解读一是，不过分享用精细美味的粮米和鱼肉。厌，"餍"的简体字，原意是吃饱，不厌即不过分饱食。解读二是，粮食舂得越精越好，肉切得越细越好，指一心享用精细美味的粮米和鱼肉。解读二是对原文的误解，但后世更常用。今取前解。

2. 脍：切得很细的鱼或肉。

【解读】

这是一篇长文的第一句话，揭示了孔子是如何遵守一些良好的饮食习惯以及他在饮食方面的一些禁忌。孔子的饮食禁忌是，他不会过多地食用美味食品。

【句例】

1. 我继续选取我所喜爱的食物，不过适当节制。食不厌精，脍不厌细，这是我的原则。

I continue to eat the foods I love, but in moderation. My principle is *never indulging in delicious food*.

2. 他凡事追求精美，对美食更是无节制。食不厌精，脍不厌细，这是他的信条。（对"食不厌精，脍不厌细"的误读。）

He is a pursuer of all exquisite things, and has an indefinite love for delicacy in particular. His faith is *never rejecting a delicious cuisine*. （A misreading of the original.）

116　是可忍，孰不可忍

If this can be tolerated, what else may not?
absolutely intolerable
如果这可以容忍，那还有什么不能容忍呢？
绝对不可容忍

【出处】

孔子谓季氏，"八佾舞于庭，是可忍，孰不可忍也？"（论语 3.1）

Speaking of Jisun, Confucius said, "He had eight ranks of dancers dance in his own court. If that could be tolerated, what else might not?"

Note: The Jisun Family had long usurped the state power and exceeded their authority to use the palace dance pattern which was for the king's exclusive use. The breach of tradition had caused great social disorder in the state and Confucius was angry about it.

【今译】

孔子谈到季氏时说，"让八排舞女在自己的宫中献舞，如果这种行为可以容忍，那还有什么不能容忍呢？"

【注释】

1. 季氏：指季孙氏家族，此处特指长期把持鲁国朝政的季氏家主季平子。

2. 八佾：佾，舞列。八佾是一种宫廷乐舞，纵横都是八名舞者，共六十四人。《周礼》规定周天子使用八佾，诸侯用六佾（四十八名舞者），卿大夫用四佾（三十二名）。季氏属正卿，只能用四佾。

【解读】

此事大约发生在鲁昭公二十五年（公元前 517 年）或之前。其时，以季平子为家主的季孙氏专横跋扈到了令人无法容忍的地步。《左传·昭公二十五年》曾记载：昭公要为襄公举行大祭，季氏却把舞者带到自己的私庙献舞，导致公室家庙的舞者仅剩两人。季氏的违礼最终导致鲁国政局大乱，这是孔子愤慨的原因。

【句例】

1. 诈骗犯连 80 岁老人都要骗。是可忍，孰不可忍？

The swindlers will even cheat an 80-year-old person. *If this can be tolerated, what else may not*?

2. 该把这些环境破坏者绳之以法了。是可忍，孰不可忍？

It's time to bring these environmental vandals to justice. It is *absolutely intolerable*!

117 逝者如斯

Time elapses just like this (river water)
(to sigh over) the swift elapse of time
时光的流逝就像这（河水）一样。
（感叹）时光易逝

【出处】

子在川上曰："逝者如斯夫，不舍昼夜。"（论语 9.17）

Watching the surging current by the riverside the Master said, "O time elapses just like this, day and night without cease!"

Note: When Confucius was standing by the riverside watching the water flowing forward swiftly and endlessly, he expressed his emotion something like "Lost time is never found again", and "Time and tide wait for no man".

【今译】

孔子站在河边感慨地说："时光的流逝就像这河水一样，不分昼夜地流淌啊！"

【注释】

1. 斯：这。此处指江水的不断流淌。

2. 舍：舍，放弃，停止。

【解读】

这段话反映孔子对韶光易逝的感慨，既有对世间一切事物盛衰兴替的感慨，也有鞭策人们珍惜光阴、只争朝夕，努力争取成就一番事业的含义。他的话也成了"时不我待"的警语。

【句例】

1. 韶光易逝，逝者如斯。我们搞城市建设，要有只争朝夕的精神。
Time elapses fast just like the river water. We should seize every hour in our

urban reconstruction.

2. 不要成天感叹逝者如斯，要学会充分利用生活中的每一分钟。

Never keep sighing over *the swift elapse of time*. Learn to make the best of every minute in your life.

118 手足无措

at a loss as to what to do
to feel (be) embarrassed
不知该怎么办
感到尴尬

【出处】

子曰·"礼乐不兴则刑罚不中, 刑罚不中, 则民无所措手足。"(论语 13.3)

The Master said, "If proprieties and music do not prevail, penalty will not be properly executed. If penalty is not properly executed, the people will be at a loss as to what to do."

Note: This is the continuation of Item 82. Confucius implied that Prince Chu still needed a licit name before he could take the throne justifiably, or he would not be able to carry out the important state administrational policies, and the people would not know what to do.

【今译】

孔子说:"礼乐制度得不到普遍施行, 刑罚的执行就不会得当。刑罚不得当, 老百姓就不知道该怎么做。"

【注释】

1. 礼乐不兴则刑罚不中: 不中, 不得当。孔子所处的时代以礼乐制度治国, 其中的礼法制度类似于当代的法律法规, 对不同阶层的人实施行为规范、教育和惩戒; 乐的作用则是用于祭祀、娱乐和教化。如果礼乐制度得不到普遍施行, 刑罚就无法恰当地执行。

2. 无所措手足: 手脚不知往哪里放, 不知该怎么做。措, 放。

【解读】

此句是第 82 条 "名正言顺" 的继续。孔子则认为卫灵公的孙子要继位, 首先要正名分。暗示他与父亲争位不对, 而这样下去, 像礼乐和刑法这样的国家大法便都无法实施，政权就难保，民众也不知道该怎么做。

【句例】

1. 一天之内士兵们接到了三个不同的命令，弄得手足无措。

In just one day the soldiers received three different orders and were *at a loss as to what to do*.

2. 如果有人请你赴家宴，千万别太早去，否则主人会被你搞的手足无措。

If someone invites you to a family dinner, never arrive too early, or it will cause the host to *be embarrassed*.

119 述而不作

to be a transmitter rather than a creator
to transmit but do not create
只传述而不创作（或创新）

【出处】

子曰："述而不作，信而好古，窃比于我老彭。"（论语 7.1）

The Master said, "I am a transmitter rather than a creator. I have belief and love in ancient things, so I venture to compare myself to my Old Peng. "

Note: Confucius was a teacher, so teaching historical documents and ancient classical works was his main task. In performing such a task he used to think of Old Peng, an ancient historian who kept to his own down-to-earth way in transmitting ancient things without creating his own things. Confucius followed this principle in his teaching and helped preserve some important original works of Chinese culture.

【今译】

孔子说："我只传述而不创作，我相信而且喜好古代文化，我私下把自己比做老彭。"

【注释】

1. 述而不作：只传述而不创作。述，传述，继承。作，创作。

2. 老彭：人名，学术界对所指何人说法不一。一指殷商时代一位好述古事的贤大夫；一指老子和彭祖二人；一指殷商时代的彭祖。今从前说。

【解读】

孔子是位老师，所以教授历史文献和古代经典著作是他的主要任务。在执行这项任务时，他经常想起古代历史学家老彭，他如实地传播古代历史知识，不创造自己的东西。孔子在教学中遵循这一原则，从而帮助保存了中国文化的一些原汁原味的著作。

【句例】

1. 多年来这位教授课堂上一向照本宣科，从不多讲自己的新东西，真是传说中的述而不作呀！

This professor keeps to his age-old teaching books in class and never adds his own new stuffs. He is exactly what they call *a transmitter rather than a creator*!

2. 孔子的述而不作在一定程度上帮助保留住一些先秦典籍的本来面目。

By transmitting the pre-Qin classics *but not creating any*, Confucius did help keep them the way they were to a certain extent.

120 死而后已

(to devote one's life to a cause) until one's death
(to work unceasingly) till the end of one's days
（为某一事业奉献终身）直到死了才停止
（不停地工作）直到生命结束

【出处】

曾子曰：“士不可以不弘毅，任重而道远。仁以为己任，不亦重乎？死而后已，不亦远乎？”（论语 8.7）

Zengzi said, "A scholar cannot but aim high and be perseverant, for he has to shoulder weighty responsibilities with a long way ahead. Isn't it weighty when he has to take it as his responsibility to help rule with benevolent governance? Isn't it long when he has to work all the way until his death?"

Note: Zengzi pointed out that a scholar should have a lofty ambition and great perseverance so as to shoulder great responsibilities in helping with state administration. And moreover, they should take it as a life-long task, working for it until the end of their days.

【今译】

曾子说：“士不可不志向远大，意志坚强，因为他肩负着重大使命，道路又很漫长。以实行仁道为己任，这副担子还不重吗？要奋斗终身，到死才停止，这条道路还不漫长吗？”

【注释】

1. 士：当时的知识分子，一般是不能继承爵禄的贵族后代，后来也有少数平民子弟通过熟习礼乐知识而成为士的。这类人不事产业，只能以自己的学识、才能和忠诚为统治阶级服务。

2. 死而后已：为自己肩负的任务而努力奋斗直至生命的终结。

【解读】

春秋晚期和战国初期，士作为治国的辅助力量已经崛起。孔子的不少学生就成了这样的士。曾子要求士要有强烈的正义感和社会责任感，要能在协助国君以德治国方面承担重任、奋斗终身。

【句例】

1. 他一生为国家的科学事业的发展而鞠躬尽瘁，死而后已。

He *devoted all his life* to the development of the national cause of science and technology. He worked hard *until his death*.

2. 这位作家的最大愿望是笔耕不止，死而后已。

The greatest wish of this writer is to write unceasingly *till the end of his days*.

121　死生有命，富贵在天

Death and life are pre-ordained by destiny; riches and ranks are bestowed by heaven.
Life and death are predetermined by heaven; riches and ranks are bestowed by heaven.
人的生死是由天命决定的

【出处】

司马牛忧曰："人皆有兄弟，我独亡。"子夏曰："商闻之矣：死生有命，富贵在天。君子敬而无失，与人恭而有礼，四海之内，皆兄弟也。君子何患乎无兄弟也？"（论语 12.5）

Anxiety-ridden, Sima Niu said, "All the others have their brothers; only I have none."

Zixia said to him, "I have heard such a saying: 'Death and life are pre-ordained by destiny; riches and ranks are bestowed by heaven.'

"If a superior man is devoted to duty and makes no errors, if in treating others he is respectful and courteous, then all men under the sun are brothers. Why should a superior man be worried about having no brothers?"

Note: Sima Niu was said to have broken off the brotherhood with his brother Huantui who rebelled and was forced into exile. Now he went to Zixia for advice as he didn't know if it was right to do that. Zixia told him to leave the matter to destiny, and try to establish brotherhood with other people.

【今译】

司马牛忧愁地说："别人都有兄弟，唯独我没有。"子夏说："我听说过：'人的生死是由命运决定的，人的富贵全靠天的赐予。'君子只要对待所做的事情严肃认真，不出差错，对人恭敬而合乎礼的规定，那么，天下人就都是自己的兄弟了。君子何愁没有兄弟呢？"

【注释】

1. 亡：音义同"无"。

2. 商：子夏姓卜名商，商是子夏的自称。

【解读】

司马牛的哥哥桓魋造反不成而出逃，司马牛曾宣布不承认他是哥哥，但内心不安，为此向同学子夏请教。子夏一面劝他听天由命放宽心，一面鼓励他谦恭有礼结交天下朋友，就不愁没有兄弟了。

【句例】

1. 他说："死生有命，富贵在天。成天怕这怕那是没用的。"

He said, "*Death and life are pre-ordained by destiny*; riches and ranks are bestowed by heaven. It's no use worrying all day about everything."

2. 虽说死生有命，但注意安全却是最要紧的。

Safety is the most important thing although they say that *life and death are predetermined by heaven*.

122　四海之内皆兄弟

All men under the sun are brothers.
Within the four seas all men are brothers.
天下人都是自己的兄弟。

【出处】

子夏曰："君子敬而无失，与人恭而有礼，四海之内，皆兄弟也。君子何患乎无兄弟也？"（论语 12.5）

Zixia said, "If a superior man is devoted to duty and makes no errors, if in treating others he is respectful and courteous, then all men under the sun are brothers. Why should a superior man be worried about having no brothers?"

Note: Sima Niu had broken off the brotherhood with his brother Huantui. He went to Zixia for advice as he didn't know if it was right to do that. Zixia told him to leave the matter to destiny, and also told him to try to establish brotherhood with other people.

【今译】

子夏说："君子只要对待所做的事情严肃认真，不出差错，对人恭敬而合乎礼的规定，那么，天下人就都是自己的兄弟了。君子何愁没有兄弟呢？"

【注释】

1. 患：担忧。

【解读】

司马牛的哥哥桓魋造反不成而出逃，司马牛曾宣布不承认他是哥哥，但内心不安，为此向同学子夏请教。子夏一面劝他听天由命放宽心，一面鼓励他谦恭有礼结交天下朋友。

【句例】

1. 四海之内皆兄弟，所以我们应该互相帮助，互相关心，互相爱护。
All men under the sun are brothers, so we should help each other, take care of

each other and love each other.

2. 四海之内皆兄弟。只要你诚恳待人，就一定能结交到好朋友。

Within the four seas all men are brothers. You are sure to have good friends so long as you are sincere to others.

123 四体不勤，五谷不分

With a sound body you are reluctant to labor and
unable to tell apart different types of grain.
neither do manual labor nor know about agriculture
空有四肢却不愿劳作，连五谷都分不清。
不从事体力活动，也不懂农业

【出处】

子路从而后，遇丈人，以杖荷蓧。子路问曰："子见夫子乎？"丈人曰："四体不勤，五谷不分，孰为夫子？"植其杖而芸。（论语 18.7）

Once Zilu lagged behind his master on a trip, and happened to meet an elderly man who was carrying on his shoulder a cane with a weeding tool on one end. Zilu went up to him and asked, "Do you happen to see my master, sir?"

The old man replied, "With a sound body you are reluctant to labor, and unable to tell apart different types of grain. Who's your master?" With those words, he inserted the cane in the field and began to weed.

Note: Zilu met an old hermit and asked the way. The old man criticized him for following Confucius in his political tour all days in vain without doing any substantial work. He didn't think the political pursuit of Confucius and his men could save the disordered world.

【今译】

子路跟随孔子出行，落在了后面，遇到一个用拐杖挑着除草工具的老人。子路问："您看到我的老师吗？"老人说："空有四肢而不愿劳作，连五谷都分不清，谁是你的老师？"说完便把拐杖插在田边开始除草。

【注释】

1. 丈人：对上了年纪的男人的尊称。
2. 蓧：古代耘田所用的竹器。
3. 芸：同"耘"，除草。

【解读】

子路遇到一个年老的隐士并向他问路。那老人批评子路成天跟着孔子周游列国，不懂农耕，不干正事，一事无成。他认为孔子师徒的政治追求无法拯救混乱的天下。

【句例】

1. 刚到农村落户时，他们只是一群四体不勤、五谷不分的中学生。

When they first settled down in the countryside, they were only middle-school students who *were reluctant to labor and unable to tell apart different types of grain*.

2. 旧知识分子大多四体不勤，五谷不分。

Most of the old-style intellectuals could *neither do manual labor nor know about agriculture*.

124 驷不及舌

A word uttered cannot be taken back even by four horses.
A word spoken can never be taken back.
一句话说出口，四匹马拉的车也追不回。
一言既出，驷马难追。

【出处】

棘子成曰："君子质而已矣，何以文为？"子贡曰："惜乎夫子之说君子也！驷不及舌。文犹质也，质犹文也，虎豹之鞟犹犬羊之鞟。"（论语 12.8）

Ji Zicheng said, "For a superior man, it is only the inner quality that matters. Why mention the exterior refinement?"

"It is a pity that you should depict a superior man that way!" said Zigong. "But a word uttered cannot be taken back even by four horses.

"Inner quality is as important as exterior refinement, and vice versa. The hide of a tiger or a leopard without the fur looks no better than that of a dog or a goat."

Note: Zi Gong politely criticized a minister of the State of Wei, saying that his speech was not thoughtful, because it was not enough for an official to have simple internal qualities, and that he should have exterior refinement so as to establish prestige.

【今译】

棘子成说："君子有好的本质就行了，要那些外在文采干什么呢？"子贡说："真遗憾，先生您这样谈论君子。但是一言既出，驷马难追。文采就像本质，本质就像文采，都是同等重要的。去掉了毛的虎豹皮，跟去掉了毛的狗皮或羊皮就没有什么不同了。"

【注释】

1. 文：指人的礼仪文采，即今人所谓有颜值、重礼仪、好口才等。

2. 驷：拉一辆车的四匹马。

3. 鞟：去掉毛的皮，即革。

【解读】

子贡婉言批评卫国大夫棘子成说话欠思量，因为负有治国责任的君子光有朴素的内在品质还不够，还要有外部的文采，才会树立威望。

【句例】

1. 你说话要谨慎。驷不及舌，后悔是来不及的。

You should be cautious in speech. *A word* wrongly *uttered cannot be taken back even by four horses*. It's too late to repent.

2. 驷不及舌，话要想好了再说

A word spoken can never be taken back, so we should think carefully before we speak.

125 岁不我与

Time and tide wait for no man.
时不我待，岁月不等人。

【出处】

　　阳货曰·"怀其宝而迷其邦，可谓仁乎？"曰："不可。""好从事而亟失时，可谓知乎？"曰："不可。""日月逝矣，岁不我与。"孔子曰："诺，吾将仕矣。"（论语17.1）

　　Yang Huo said, "Can he be considered virtuous if he treasures up his talents only to leave his state in disorder?" "No, he can't" replied Confucius. "Can he be considered wise if he is anxious to be engaged in government, and yet constantly losing the opportunities?" Yang Huo asked again and Confucius said, "No." "Days and months go by quickly. Time and tide wait for no man," urged Yang. "All right. I will go into office," said Confucius.

Note: Yang Huo usurped the state power and incited Confucius to join him with the above sweet words. Confucius first pretended to agree to consider it and refused to join him eventually.

【今译】

　　阳货说："身怀本领而听任国家陷入迷乱，这可以叫做仁吗？"孔子回答说："不可以。"（阳货）说："喜欢参与政事而又屡次错过机会，这可以说是智吗？"（孔子回答）说："不可以。"（阳货）说："时间一天天过去了，岁月是不等人的。"孔子说："好吧，我要出来做官了。"

【注释】

　　1. 阳货：又称阳虎，季氏家臣。

　　2. 迷其邦：听任国家陷入混乱。

　　3. 亟：屡次。

【解读】

阳虎囚禁鲁相季桓子，实际上控制了鲁国的大权。为了扩大势力，他花言巧语想引诱孔子入伙。孔子虚与委蛇，最终拒绝加盟。

【句例】

1. 时不我待，岁不我与。吾辈须趁年轻精进自强。

Time and tide wait for no men. We young people should strive for self-fulfilment before it is too late.

2. 许多人都懂得岁不我与，却很少有人争分夺秒去实现人生的目标。

Many people know that *time and tide wait for no men*, but there are few who can race against the clock to achieve their life goals.

126　岁寒知松柏

Only in cold winter months do we find that the pine
and cypress are the last to wither.
Adversity tests men and reveals virtue.
只有到了一年中的寒冷季节，才知道松柏是不会凋萎的。
逆境考验人、显美德。

【出处】

子曰："岁寒，然后知松柏之后凋也。"（论语 9.28）

The Master said, "Only in cold winter months do we find that the pine and cypress are the last to wither."

Note: Confucius pointed out that rigorous circumstances could test a man's will power, and he hoped that people would foster their staunch spirit and strong character in adversity.

【今译】

孔子说："只有到了一年中的寒冷季节，才知道松柏是不会凋萎的。"

【注释】

1. 岁寒：天冷之时。这里借指乱世或艰难时世。

2. 松柏：松树和柏树。这里借指具有君子人格的人。

【解读】

此句讲寒冬腊月，方知松柏常青。孔子借用当时熟语，比喻只有经过严峻的考验，才能看出一个人的品质，也说明艰苦的环境更能考验一个人的坚贞。"岁寒知松柏"从此成为中国人千古传诵的名言。

【句例】

1. 岁寒知松柏。现在你们在最艰苦的时刻守卫着祖国的边关，一定要经得起考验。

Only in cold winter months do we find that the pine and cypress are the last to wither. Now you are experiencing the hardest time to guard the border of our country, and must stand the test.

2. 岁寒知松柏，逆境考验人。这支部队是从艰苦的环境中锤炼出来的，因而是战无不胜的。

Adversity tests men and reveals virtue. This troop has been forged on the anvil of a harsh environment and it is invincible.

127 听其言而观其行

to observe what one does while listening to what he says
to judge a person by his deeds, not just by his words
听了他讲的话还要观察他的行为

【出处】

子曰："始吾于人也，听其言而信其行；今吾于人也，听其言而观其行。予予与改是。"（论语 5.10）

The Master said, "First, to a man, I used to listen to his words and believe in his deeds. "Now, to a man, I will pay regard to what he does while listening to what he says. It is Yu that has caused me to change my way."

Note: This is the continuation of 143 (Rotten wood cannot be carved). Confucius not only criticized Zai Yu (Zai Wo) for his sleeping in the day time, but also declared that he would no longer believe in Zai Yu's words so easily.

【今译】

孔子说："起初我对一个人，是听了他说的话便相信了他的行为；现在我对一个人，听了他讲的话还要观察他的行为。是宰予这个人改变了我观察人的方法。"

【注释】

1. 予：宰予，孔子的弟子，又称宰我。

【解读】

此句是后面"朽木不可雕"（见 143 条）的继续，讲的是孔子对学生宰予（宰我）白天睡觉的批评。孔子一向强调学习的重要性，把好学看成做人的一大美德，所以才对他的行为那么生气。宰予能言善辩，话说得好听，孔子则说，以后要先观察他的行动，不能光听了他的话便相信他，还说要把这也用到别人身上。

【句例】

1. 在重大问题上不能轻信一个人。最好先听其言而观其行。

Never believe in a person so easily on important matters. We had better *first observe what he does while listening to what he says*.

2. 听其言而观其行有助于我们更好地与别人开展合作。

Judging people by their deeds but not merely by their words will help us to cooperate with them better.

128 危言危行

to be upright in speech and upright in action
说话要正直，行为要正直

【出处】

子曰：“邦有道，危言危行；邦无道，危行言孙。”（论语 14.3）

The Master said, "When good government prevails in a state, be upright in speech and upright in action. When bad government prevails in a state, be upright in action but cautious in speech."

Note: According to Confucius, if good governance prevails in a state, upright words and actions will benefit the state and not bring disaster to one, but when bad governance prevails in a state, one should maintain upright in action, meaning not to do evil things, but he should be cautious in speech less he should incur disaster. This should be a tactic in one's effort to achieve a certain lofty goal, especially in a dangerous political environment.

【今译】

孔子说：“国家政治清明，说话要正直，行为要正直；国家政局颓败，行为要正直，但说话要谨慎。”

【注释】

1. 危言：直言。危，正直的。又如“正襟危坐”，危意为端正的。
2. 危行：做正直的事。
3. 言孙：说话要低调。孙，同“逊”。

【解读】

孔子认为国家政治清明时，言行正直对国家有利又不会给自身招来灾祸。国家政局颓败时，行为照样要正直（意思是不干坏事），但说话要小心，以免招祸。这应该是一个人在努力实现某个崇高目标时的策略，尤其是在危险的政治环境中更应如此。

【句例】

1. 如果一个国家政治清明，危言危行倒无大碍。

If good governance prevails in a country, being *upright in speech and upright in action* won't do one much harm.

2. 身处乱世最好是危行言逊。他那样危言危行恐怕有麻烦。

It's better to be *upright in action but cautious in speech* in a chaotic country. He may get into trouble as he is *upright in speech and upright in action*.

129 枉道事人

to serve the state ruler in crooked ways (originally)
to serve others in crooked ways (a variant today)
违背正道事奉国君（原意）
违背正道事奉他人（今意）

【出处】

柳下惠为士师，三黜。人曰："子未可以去乎？"曰："直道而事人，焉往而不三黜？枉道而事人，何必去父母之邦？"（论语 18.2）

Liuxia Hui once acted as a chief criminal judge. Knowing that he was dismissed from his post three times, some said to him, "Can't you leave this state?"

"Where can I go without being dismissed many times when I serve a prince righteously?" responded Liuxia. "And what need would there be to leave my motherland if I served the prince in crooked ways?"

Note: Liuxia Hui was dismissed from office many times because of his integrity, but he still adhered to the principle and never turned to serve the state ruler in crooked ways. He would not leave his home state simply because he was wrongly treated. Instead, he would stay to serve the state and people although that might mean humiliation and hard work to him. He remained undefiled in spite of the corrupted society.

【今译】

柳下惠当典狱官，多次被罢免。有人说："你不可以离开鲁国吗？"柳下惠说："按正道服事君主，到哪里不会被多次罢官呢？如果违背正道服事君主，那又何必要离开我的祖国呢？"

【注释】

1. 柳下惠：名展获，鲁国贤大夫。
2. 士师：典狱官，掌管刑狱。
3. 三黜：多次被罢免。黜，罢免。
4. 枉道：歪门邪道，不正当的手段。

【解读】

柳下惠因正直而多次被罢官，但仍然坚持原则，决不枉道事君。他不会因为遭受不公的对待而离开故国，而是留下来，为国为民忍辱负重，认真为官做好本职工作，身处污泥而不染。

【句例】

1. 他是一位正直的宰相，绝不枉道事人。

He was an upright prime minister. Never would he *serve the emperor in crooked ways*.

2. 他不愿枉道事人，毅然离开那个专制的执行总裁统治下的公司。

He didn't want to *serve others in crooked ways*, and resolutely left the company under the autocratic CEO.

130 温故而知新

to review what has been learned to perceive what is new
to sum up past experience so as to know about new things
温习旧知识，获得新的领悟
总结过去的经验，了解新的情况

【出处】

子曰："温故而知新，可以为师矣。"（论语 2.11）

The Master said, "Review what you have learned to perceive what is new, and you will be qualified to be a teacher."

Note: Confucius encouraged his disciples to review the old knowledge so as to explore and perceive the new.

【今译】

孔子说："复习所学的知识，从中获得新的领悟，努力吸收新知，就有资格当老师了。"

【注释】

1. 故：旧知识，学过的知识。

2. 知：知道，了解，领悟，发现。

3. 新：新的知识。

【解读】

孔子提出"温故而知新"的学习方法，影响了中国两千多年，是对我国教育学的重大贡献之一。"知新"在这里包含两个层面。一是从旧知识中获得新的领悟。人类认识世界，是一个连贯的、由浅入深、由微及显的过程。人们的新知识、新学问往往都是在过去所学知识的基础上发展而来的，因此，温故而知新是一个完全符合人类认知规律的学习方法。二是努力吸收新知识，接受新事物，而作为一名老师，同样必须循序渐进地把学生引入新的知识天地。总之，只有做到这两条，才有资格成为一名教师。

【句例】

1. 温故而知新是儒家的教学原则。

Reviewing *what has been learned to perceive what is new* is the teaching principle of the Confucian School.

2. 公司以往的成功经验非常重要，我们现在确实有必要来个温故而知新。

The company's past successful experience is very important, so now we do need to *sum up the past experience so as to know about the new things*.

131　温良恭俭让

temperate, amicable, courteous, modest and self-effacing
temperate, kind, courteous, restrained and magnanimous
温和、友善、恭谨、谦虚、礼让

【出处】

子禽问于子贡曰：夫子至于是邦也，必闻其政，求之与，抑与之与？"子贡曰："夫子温、良、恭、俭、让以得之。夫子之求之也，其诸异乎人之求之与？"（论语 1.10）

Ziqin asked Zigong, "Whenever he gets to a state, our master will be told about its government affairs. Does he seek such an honor, or do they offer him the honor instead?"

"Our master is temperate, amicable, courteous, modest and self-effacing, with which he seeks the honor," replied Zigong. "Our master's seeking is different from that of others, isn't it?"

Note: Ziqin found that Confucius would be told about a state's affairs no matter which state he went to. He wondered whether this honor was given by the state rulers or was it sought by Confucius, so he asked his fellow disciple Zigong. Zigong told him that it was with his excellent personality that their teacher, Confucius, had won himself respect and trust from many state rulers.

【今译】

子禽问子贡说："老师到了一个国家，总是被告知这个国家的政事。（这种荣耀）是他自己求得的呢，还是人家主动给他的呢？"子贡说："老师温和、友善、恭谨、谦逊、礼让，所以才求得到这样的荣耀，但他的求，大概跟别人的求有所不同吧？"

【注释】

1. 子禽：姓陈名亢（gāng），孔子的学生。一说非孔子学生。

2. 闻其政：与（预）闻政事，即被告知该国政事并发表自己的见解，这是诸侯国君对德高望重的外来学者的信任和礼遇。

【解读】

这段话记孔子弟子对孔子人格魅力的崇敬及对这种人格魅力成因的探讨。子禽发现老师不论走到哪个诸侯国，都能与闻该国政事，不知道这种荣耀是诸侯国君主动给予的，还是老师求来的，所以才问同学子贡。子贡解释时以退为进，先说老师的荣耀是求来的，然后说老师是靠温、良、恭、俭、让的高尚人格魅力赢得尊重和信赖，暗示这种荣耀其实不是老师"求"来的，而是诸侯国君主动给他的。

【句例】

1. 他这个人温、良、恭、俭、让，但决不是一个好好先生。

He is *temperate, amicable, courteous, modest and self-effacing*, but is absolutely not a goody-goody.

2 救灾不是请客吃饭，不能那样温、良、恭、俭、让。

Disaster relief is not a dinner party. You should not be so *temperate, kind, courteous, restrained and magnanimous* in it.

132　文武之道

the Way (doctrine) of King Wen and King Wu (original)
the combination of exertion and relaxation (a variant today)
周文王和周武王的治国之道（原意）
一张一弛，劳逸结合（今意）

【出处】

子贡口："文武之道，未坠于地，在人。贤者识其大者，不贤者识其小者，莫不有义武之道焉。夫子焉不学？而亦何常师之有？"（论语 19.22）

Zigong said, "The doctrines of King Wen and King Wu have not yet fallen into ruin. They are still found among people. Those who are of worthy quality grasp the major principles of them, and those inferior grasp the minor, all possessing the doctrines of King Wen and King Wu. Where could our Master go without an opportunity of learning them? And what need is there for him to have a regular teacher?"

Note: Someone asked where Confucius learned his theory of state governing. Zigong said Confucius learned the way from King Wen and King Wu of the Zhou Dynasty. He also said that in Confucius' time, the way of King Wen and King Wu had not been completely lost, so Confucius could learn from those who knew about it. Confucius had no regular teacher and was not ashamed to learn from those who were inferior to him, so he became knowledgeable and was widely respected.

【今译】

子贡说："文王和武王的治国之道并没有失传，还留在人们中间。贤能的人了解它的根本，不够贤能的人了解它的细节，在他们身上无不都有文王武王之道。我们老师哪儿学不到，何必一定要有固定的老师呢？"

【注释】

1. 文武之道：周文王和周武王的治国之道，也指治国要宽严结合。后世比喻生活工作要有张有弛，劳逸结合。

【解读】

有人问孔子的治国理论是哪里学来的。子贡说孔子学的是周文王和周武王的治国之道。他还说，在孔子时代，文武之道还没有完全失传，所以孔子可以向了解它的人学习。孔子学无常师，不耻下问，所以才能做到博学多闻，受人敬重。

【句例】

1. 文武之道是周王朝的治国方针。

The Way of King Wen and King Wu was the ruling principle of the Zhou Dynasty.

2. 文武之道，一张一弛。紧张与放松相结合，工作学习才能持久。

The energy of learning and working can only be sustainable through *the combination of exertion and relaxation.*

133 文质彬彬

the proper combination of exterior refinement with plain nature
being refined and elegant
内在的质朴和外在的文采恰当地配合起来
文雅

【出处】

子曰："质胜文则野，文胜质则史。文质彬彬，然后君子。"（论语 6.18）

The Master said, "When his plain nature prevails over his exterior refinement, a man appears coarse; when his exterior refinement outshines his plain nature, he appears flashy. The proper combination of exterior refinement with plain nature helps make a true superior man."

Note: Confucius pointed out that a superior man (usually a high-ranking official) should possess both plain inner quality and exterior refinement, and it was believed that in this way they could build prestige and their ruling would be made easier.

【今译】

孔子说："质朴多于文采，就流于粗俗；文采多于质朴，就流于花俏。只有把内在的质朴和外在的文采恰当地配合起来，才是个君子。"

【注释】

1. 质：质朴，指人的朴素的本质。

2. 文：指人的礼仪文采，即今人所谓有颜值、重礼仪、好口才等。

3. 史：原指掌管文案的小官。这类人文采飞扬、但花俏、不实。

4. 彬彬：配合得很恰当。文质彬彬，指把内在的质朴和外在的文采恰当地配合起来。后世借指一个人很文雅。

【解读】

在孔子看来，君子为政，内在的质朴和外表的高雅恰当配合往往意味着更为成功的领导效果。孔子办学的目的之一是要培养一批从政的君子。他的学生大多出身贫寒，普遍质朴有余而文采不足，故孔子除文化传授外，也希望他们做好文与质的恰当结合。

【句例】

1. 古代要求当官的做到文质彬彬，以便树立威望。

Officials of ancient times were required to *combine their exterior refinement with plain nature properly* so as to build prestige.

2. 他只是工厂里的一名蓝领工人，外表却是文质彬彬的。

He is only a blue-collar worker at the factory, but he looks so *refined and elegant*.

134 闻一知十

From one instance one is told, he can
draw inferences about ten other cases.
to infer the whole matter after hearing only one point
听到一件事就可以推知十件事
听到一件事就可以推知整件事

【出处】

　　子谓子贡曰："女与回也孰愈？"对曰："赐也何敢望回？回也闻一以知十，赐也闻一以知二。"子曰："弗如也。吾与女弗如也。"（论语 5.9）

　　The Master asked Zigong, "Which do you consider better, you or Hui?"

　　"How dare I compare myself with Hui?" replied Zigong. "From one instance he is told, Hui will draw inferences about ten other cases, while I, only two."

　　"It's true that you are not as good as him," said the Master. "I agree that you are not as good as him."

Note: Yan Hui (Yan Yuan) and Zigong were both excellent disciples of Confucius. Zigong said Yan Hui could draw inferences about ten cases from one instance he was told because he had excellent understanding capacity. Confucius agreed with Zigong. This shows that Confucius favored Yan Hui more.

【今译】

　　孔子对子贡说："你和颜回两个相比，谁更好些呢？"子贡回答说："我怎么敢和颜回相比呢？颜回听到一件事就可以推知十件事；我呢，知道一件事，只能推知两件事。"孔子说："你是不如他呀，我同意你说的，你不如他。"

【注释】

　　1. 孰愈：谁胜过（谁）。孰，谁；愈，胜过、超过。

　　2. 与：赞同、同意。

【解读】

　　颜回和子贡都是孔子的优秀弟子。子贡说，颜回能闻一知十，因为他有很强的理解能力。孔子同意子贡的观点。由此可见孔子对颜回的喜爱程度更高。

【句例】

1. 他悟性极强，能闻一知十。

He is a man of great understanding. *From one instance he is told, he can draw inferences about ten other cases.*

2. 要解决这个难题，你们须要有闻一知十的推理能力。

To solve this difficult problem, you need to have *the ability of inferring the whole matter after hearing only one point.*

135 无可无不可

There is nothing that one ought to do or ought not to do.
to take an indifferent attitude (a variant now)
没有一定可做或一定不可做的事
对事情抱无所谓态度（后世变异）

【出处】

子曰："我则异于是，无可无不可。"（论语 18.8）

The Master said, "I am different from all of them. There is nothing I ought to do or ought not to do."

Note: Before this sentence, Confucius evaluated three different types of people, and said he was different from them. He would not force himself to be an official, nor would he retreat blindly as a hermit. His principle was that if the state needed him, he would take office; otherwise he would retire to do what he liked. He would not force himself to do one thing or not to do the other. At the age of 54, Confucius traveled around many states and began to seek opportunities to save the disordered world. At the age of 68 when he realized that his political tour had been fruitless, he returned to his homeland and continued his teaching career, gradually staying out of political affairs. He acted exactly in accordance with this principle.

【今译】

孔子说："我却与这些人不同，没有一定可做或一定不可做的事。"

【注释】

1. 无可无不可：没有绝对固定可以做或不可以做的事。后世也用来指做事无主见，抱无所谓的态度。

【解读】

这句话的前面讲到了孔子对几种类型的人物进行分析、对比、评价，最后指出自己跟他们不同，不会像有些人强求入仕，也不会像另一些人盲目隐退。他的原则是，社会需要他，他会勇敢地挑起重任，社会不能用他，他就引退去做自己喜欢的事。孔子 54 岁时周游列国，开始了寻求救世的机会，68 岁时发现自己的政治游历无果，便返回祖国，继续他的教书和修书生涯，逐渐不问政事，体现的正是这一原则。

【句例】

1. 我的原则是根据具体情况决定自己的行动，无可无不可。

My principle is to determine my actions in accordance with specific circumstances. *There is nothing I ought to do or ought not to do*.

2. 对原则问题不应采取无可无不可的态度。

One should not *take an indifferent attitude* toward issues of principle.

136 无为而治

to rule by doing nothing
the policy of inaction
to take the non-interference policy
（君主）无所作为而使天下得到良性治理
采取不干涉政策

【出处】

子曰："无为而治者，其舜也与？夫何为哉？恭己正南面而已矣。"（论语15.5）

The Master said, "Shun might be the one who ruled by doing nothing, wasn't he? What did he do then? He was just seated in the throne solemnly and rightly."

Note: Confucius highly praised Shun, a remote ancient sage king, for ruling his dominion and people very well by means of non-interference policy, with his exemplary role in morality to mobilize the subjective initiative of his subordinates and the people to do their part well.

【今译】

孔子说："能做到无为而治的，大概只有舜吧？他做了些什么呢？他只是庄严端正地坐在朝廷的王位上罢了。"

【注释】

1. 无为而治：君主无所作为而使天下得到治理。原指舜当政的时候，沿袭尧的主张，不做丝毫改变。后泛指儒家提倡的君主以德化民，使政治清明，社会安定，激励民众奋发自为的统治方法。也指管理上采取不干涉政策。

2. 恭己：指君主提高道德修养使自己态度庄重、举止端正。

3. 正南面：端正地坐在王位上。南面，古时帝王和官员临朝、视事时均面向南而坐。正，就是以德立身，使自己的思想言行达到正己以正人的目的，安其位而起表率作用。

【解读】

孔子提倡的"无为而治"与道家主张不同，他强调国君应该首先克己修身崇德（恭己），然后举贤任能，顺应人性，让下属和百姓各司其职，各尽所能，不横加干涉，不好大喜功劳民伤财，达到不用事必躬亲而政治清明、社会安定、人民安居乐业的结果。

【句例】

1. 由于皇帝采取无为而治的政策，二十年后财富堆满了整个天下。

Due to the emperor's policy of inaction, wealth piled up throughout the empire twenty years later.

2. 在经济管理上采取无为而治的政策将有助于保持市场经济的健康发展。

Taking the non-interference policy in economic management will help to maintain the healthy development of the market economy.

137　贤贤易色

to value the virtuous more than a man does a beauty
to value virtues more than beauty
尊重贤明的人胜过重女色
重贤德，轻女色

【出处】

子夏曰："贤贤易色；事父母能竭其力；事君，能致其身；与朋友交，言而有信。虽曰未学，吾必谓之学矣。"（论语 1.7）

Zixia said, "If a man values the virtuous more than he does a beauty, if he does his utmost in serving his parents, if he can dedicate his life to serving his prince, if he is faithful in word among friends, I certainly consider him a good learner, though others might think otherwise."

Note: According to Confucius, reading and learning is the most important way for one to cultivate himself and stand in the world. But Zixia had a unique view on learning, that is, practice is also learning. The practice here refers to the respect for the virtuous, the loyalty to the monarch, the filial piety to parents and good faith to friends.

【今译】

子夏说："一个人能够尊重贤明的人而不看重女色；侍奉父母能尽心竭力；服事君主能不惜献身；同朋友交往，说话诚实、恪守信用。这样的人，尽管有人说他没有学习过，我一定说他已经学习过了。"

【注释】

1. 子夏：姓卜名商，字子夏，卫国人。孔子晚年弟子。

2. 贤贤：敬重贤明之人。第一个贤为动词，敬重；第二个贤是名词，即贤者。

3. 易色：看轻姿色，不重女色。

4. 致：奉献。

－269－

【解读】

按孔子的说法，读书和学习是一个人修养和立足于世界的最重要的方式。但子夏对读书学习有独特的见解，即实践也是学习。这里的实践是指对贤人的尊重，对君主的忠诚，对父母的孝顺和对朋友的诚信。

【句例】

1. 贤贤易色应该成为一个公司选拔人员的主要标准。

Valuing the virtuous more than a man does a beauty should be the main criterion for a company when it selects personnel.

2. 贤贤易色应该成为一个男人择偶的主要标准。

Valuing virtues more than beauty should be the main criterion for a man when he selects a spouse.

138　小不忍则乱大谋

A lack of forbearance in small matters spoils a great plan.
A little impatience spoils a great plan.
小事不忍耐，就会败坏大事。

【出处】

子曰："巧言乱德。小不忍则乱大谋。"（论语 15.27）

The Master said, "Artful talks ruin one's virtue. A lack of forbearance in small matters spoils a great plan."

Note: On the one hand, Confucius said he disliked sweet words; on the other hand, he pointed out that in order to achieve a great goal, one should guard against irrationally excessive reaction to small insults or setbacks.

【今译】

孔子说："花言巧语会败坏德行，小事不忍耐，就会败坏大事。"

【注释】

1. 大谋：大事。

【解读】

孔子的这段名言是做大事、成大事者的座右铭。做大事的人所遇到的事情必然纷繁复杂，故抓大事显得尤为重要。能成大事的人，要能分清轻重主次，善于隐忍，不能在小事上失去自控力，打乱原来的部署和谋略，致使功败垂成。

【句例】

1. 如果你想成就大事，就必须学会在小事上忍辱。切记小不忍则乱大谋。

If you want to accomplish something great, you must learn to endure small insults. Remember that *a lack of forbearance in small matters spoils a great plan*.

2. 小不忍则乱大谋。我们应当理性对待他人的一些小误解和冒犯，始终不忘自己的大目标。

A little impatience spoils a great plan. We should rationally treat others' minor misunderstandings and offenses, and always bear in mind our great goal ahead.

139 小知大受

be assigned to a minor task or be entrusted with a great mission
to assign different tasks to different people
任用于小事或承担重大的使命
让不同的人承担不同的任务

【出处】

子曰："君子不可小知而可大受也，小人不可大受而可小知也。"（论语 15.34）

The Master said, "A superior man should not be assigned to a minor task, but can be entrusted with a great mission. An ordinary man should not be entrusted with a grand mission, but can be assigned to a minor task."

Note: Confucius pointed out that those in higher positions and the common people should be given different tasks, because the former had the opportunities and abilities to should great responsibilities, while the latter had the skills and abilities to do practical work. This reflects his sense of the social division of labor.

【今译】

孔子说："君子不可以任用于小事，却可以承担重大的使命。小人不能承担重大的使命，却可以任用于小事。"

【注释】

1. 小知：做小事情，管理小事。知，主政、管理。旧时县长称为知县，就是主政管理一个县的意思。

2. 大受：承担大任。

【解读】

孔子指出，身居高位的人和普通人应该被赋予不同的任务，因为前者有机会和能力承担重大责任，而后者有技能和能力做实际工作。这反映了他对社会分工的认识。

【句例】

1. "君子不可小知而可大受也"反映了古代中国社会分工的不同。

That a superior man *should not be assigned to a minor task but can be entrusted with a great mission* reflected the differences in social division of labor in ancient China.

2. 小知大受这个社会分工原则在我们今天仍然是有效的。

The principle of social division of labor known as *assigning different tasks to different people* is still valid today.

140 信而好古

to believe in ancient things and love them
相信并喜好古代的东西

【出处】

子曰："述而不作，信而好古，窃比于我老彭。"（论语7.1）

The Master said, "I am a transmitter rather than a creator. I believe in ancient things and love them, so I venture to compare myself to my Old Peng."

Note: Confucius was a teacher, so teaching historical documents and ancient classical works was his main task. In performing such a task he used to think of Old Peng, an ancient historian who kept to his own down-to-earth way in transmitting ancient culture without creating his own things. On this principle Confucius helped preserve some important original works of traditional Chinese culture. And he did the same in teaching the ideas of governance and social philosophy.

【今译】

孔子说："我只传述而不创作，我相信并喜好古代文化，我私下把自己比做老彭。"

【注释】

1. 窃：私下里。

2. 老彭：孔子之前的一位历史学家，具体不详。

【解读】

孔子是位老师，教授历史文献和古代经典著作是他的主要任务。在执行这项任务时，他经常想起老彭这位古代历史学家，他如实地传播古代文化而不创作自己东西的。根据这一原则，孔子帮助保存了中国传统文化的一些重要原本。在传授治国方略和社会哲学思想方面他也是这样做的。

【句例】

1. 他这个人信而好古，可以当一名文史研究员。

He *believes in ancient things and love them*, so he can make a history researcher.

2. 信而好古没错，但也不能一味迷信古人。

It's all right for one to *believe in ancient things and love them,* but he must not blindly believe in the ancients.

141 行不由径

never resort to any crooked means
never take a short cut
不搞歪门邪道
不走捷径

【出处】

　　子游为武城宰。子曰："女得人焉尔乎？"曰："有澹台灭明者，行不由径，非公事，未尝至于偃之室也。"（论语 6.14）

When Ziyou (Yan Yan) acted as governor of Wucheng, the Master asked him, "Have you acquired talented staff there?"

"Yes," replied Ziyou, "I've got one called Tantai Mieming. He never resorts to any crooked means, and never comes to my house except on public business."

Note: Tantai Mieming was upright, virtuous and talented. He admired Confucius and eventually became his disciple. But he looked ugly, so first Confucius looked down upon him, and later felt ashamed for that. Ziyou used Tantai Mieming and admired him for his not resorting to any crooked means in association with his superiors. This showed that Ziyou himself was also an upright official.

【今译】

　　子游做了武城的长官。孔子说："你在那里得到了人才没有？"。子游回答说："有一个叫澹台灭明的人，从来不走歪门邪道，没有公事从不到我屋子里来。"

【注释】

　　1. 澹台灭明：姓澹台名灭明，字子羽，武城人，孔子弟子。
　　2. 行不由径：走路不抄近路，比喻不走歪门邪道。径，小路。
　　3. 偃：姓言名偃，字子游，此处为自呼其名。

【解读】

　　孔子来到弟子子游当官的地方，问他是否得人才。子游为老师介绍了澹台灭明这位正直无私的同学兼下属，尤其突出他在与上级交往时从不走歪门邪道。从这里也可以看出子游本身也是个光明正大的官员。澹台灭明曾为孔子弟子，因长相丑陋，受到孔子嫌弃，后刻苦修习，学成后设教南方，从者三百多，品德才干传遍各诸侯国。孔子慨叹："我凭长相判断，看错了子羽"。

【句例】

1. 他这个人行不由径，不会有事没事去巴结上司。

He has *never resorted to any crooked means*, so he will not find excuses to curry favour with his superior.

2. 咱们行不由径。求职的事，还是照章办事，耐心等待。

Let's not *take a short cut* in applying for the job. We had better follow the regular procedures and wait patiently.

142　修己安人

Cultivate yourself so as to appease the subordinates.
Cultivate yourself so as to appease the people.
做好自我修养，使下属得到安宁。（原意）
做好自我修养，使天下百姓得到安宁。（今意）

【出处】

　　子路问君子。子曰："修己以敬。"曰："如斯而已乎？"曰："修己以安人。"曰："如斯而已乎？"曰："修己以安百姓。修己以安百姓，尧舜其犹病诸。"（论语 14.42）

　　When Zilu asked how to be a superior man, the Master said, "Cultivate yourself and work seriously."

"Is that all?" asked Zilu.

"Cultivate yourself so as to appease the subordinates," replied the Master.

"So that's enough?" again asked Zilu.

"Cultivate yourself so as to bring peace to the common people," the Master continued. "Even Yao and Shun might find it hard to manage it."

Note: Confucius pointed out that those in high positions should cultivate themselves and make it their goal to bring peace and happiness to his subordinates and the common people. Confucius also pointed out that this was worth doing although it was hard work.

【今译】

　　子路问怎样才能成为君子。孔子说："做好自我修养，办事严肃认真。"子路说："这样就够了吗？"孔子说："做好自我修养，让下属各安其位。"子路说："这样就够了吗？"孔子说："做好自我修养，使天下百姓都安宁。做好自我修养使天下百姓都安宁，连尧舜都还怕难于做到呢？"

【注释】

　　1. 安人：让下属官员各安其位。安，安抚；人，指国君周围的人。

　　2. 安百姓：使老百姓安宁。

【解读】

孔子对弟子子路谈到作为统治者的君子必须达到的三个层次。一是做好自我修养,认真执政;第二是要让属下人员安定满意,做好各自的工作。子路觉得这两个层次还不够高,孔子便提出了第三个层次,就是让天下的百姓都安宁,并指出其难度相当大。

【句例】

1. 古代好帝王往往能修己安人。

A good emperor in ancient times could usually *cultivate himself so as to appease his subordinates*.

2. 在任何社会,修己安人应该成为为官的目标。

To cultivate oneself so as to appease the people should be the goal of an official in any society.

143 朽木不可雕

Rotten wood cannot be carved.
a hopeless, worthless person (or stuff)
腐烂的木头无法雕刻。
毫无希望的无用之人（或物）

【出处】

宰予昼寝，子曰："朽木不可雕也，粪土之墙不可杇也，于予与何诛！"子曰："始吾于人也，听其言而信其行；今吾于人也，听其言而观其行。于予与改是。"（论语5.10）

When he saw Zai Yu sleep during the daytime, the Master said, "Rotten wood cannot be carved; a wall of dirt cannot be whitewashed. What is the use of my scolding him?" "At first, to a man," added the Master, "I used to listen to his words and believe in his deeds. "Now, to a man, I will pay regard to what he does while listening to what he says. It is Yu that has caused me to change my way."

Note: Confucius sternly criticized Zai Yu (Zai Wo) for his sleeping in the day time, implying that he was a worthless person that could not be used. Fortunately, Zai Yu accepted Confucius' criticism and later became one of his important and outstanding disciples.

【今译】

宰予白天睡觉。孔子说："腐朽的木头无法雕刻，脏土垒的墙壁无法粉刷。对于宰予这个人，责备还有什么用呢？"孔子说："起初我对他人，是听了他说的话便相信了他的行为；现在我对他人，听了他讲的话还要观察他的行为。是宰予这个人改变了我观察人的方法。"

【注释】

1. 昼寝：大白天睡觉。
2. 杇：抹墙用的抹子。这里指用抹子粉刷墙壁。

【解读】

此句讲孔子对学生宰予白天睡觉的批评。孔子一向强调学习的重要性，把好学看成为人的一大美德。宰予能言善辩，思维活跃，但他白天睡大觉而不能利用大好时光读书，的确让孔子十分生气，才会如此声色俱厉。还好，宰予接受了孔子的批评，日后成了孔子的一名重要的优秀弟子。

【句例】

1. 他年轻时被说成朽木不可雕，如今可是一家人工智能公司的顶级技师。

When young he was described as *a rotten wood that could not be carved*, but now he is a top technician with an AI company.

2. 这份设计方案简直是朽木不可雕。我看不出有什么修改的必要。

This design is simply *a hopeless, worthless stuff*. I don't see any need for change.

144　学而不厌　诲人不倦

to study without satiety
to be insatiable in learning
学习从不满足
（见 049）

【出处】

　　子曰："默而识之，学而不厌，诲人不倦，何有于我哉？"（论语 7.2）

The Master said, "Learning by heart and bearing in mind what is learned, studying without satiety and teaching without weariness — what difficulty is there for me to do so?"

Note: Confucius' self-evaluation is that he kept studying without satiety. That was true to the fact of his life. He was always insatiable in learning.

【今译】

　　孔子说："默默记住所学知识，学习从不满足，教书育人不知疲倦，这些对我来说有什么难呢？"

【注释】

　　1. 识：同"志"，"记住"的意思。

　　2. 厌：繁体字同"餍"，原意为饱食，此处指满足。不厌即不满足、不自满。

　　3. 何有：何难之有。

【解读】

　　孔子以学而不厌和诲人不倦自许，完全符合他一生的事实。他从不满足于他所学的东西。

【句例】

　　1. 学而不厌让他在学术研究方面一直领先于其同行。

He *studied without satiety*, which kept him ahead of his peers in academic researches.

2. 一个人责任心强，又有崇高抱负，那他从来都是学而不厌的。

A man with a strong sense of responsibility and a lofty ambition will *always be insatiable in learning*.

145　学而时习之

to learn and constantly practice what is learnt
学习知识并且时常研习

【出处】

子曰："学而时习之，不亦说乎？有朋自远方来，不亦乐乎？人不知而不愠，不亦君子乎？"（论语 1.1）

The Master said, "Isn't it a pleasure to learn and constantly practice what is learnt? Isn't it delightful to have friends coming from afar? Isn't he a gentleman who is not annoyed for not being understood?"

Note: This is the first sentence of the *Analects of Confucius*. Confucius called upon his disciples to learn and practice what they learned from time to time. And more importantly, he hoped that his disciples would take learning as a pleasure.

【今译】

孔子说："学习了知识并且时常加以研习，不是一件很愉快的事吗？有朋友从远方来，不也是很令人高兴吗？不为他人所了解也不恼怒，这样的人不也是个君子吗？"

【注释】

1. 说：通"悦"。高兴，喜悦。
2. 愠：恼火。音 yùn。

【解读】

孔子号召他的弟子不时地学习和实践他们所学到的东西。更重要的是，他希望他的弟子把学习当成一种乐趣。

【句例】

1. 学而时习之，这是最基本的学习方法。
To learn and constantly practice what is learnt is the most fundamental study

method.

2. 只有做到学而时习之，才能把知识记得牢、用得好。

Only by *learning and constantly practicing what is learned* can we remember and use the knowledge well.

146　学而优则仕　仕而优则学

A scholar with spare energy may seek to be an official.
One who studies excellently must seek to be an official. (a variant)
An official may devote his spare energy to learning.
学习有余力的人可以当官。
学习优秀的人可以当官。（背离原文）
做官还有余力的人可以去读书学习。

【出处】

子夏曰："仕而优则学，学而优则仕。"（论语 19.13）

Zixia said, "An official may devote his spare energy to learning, while a scholar with spare energy may seek to be an official."

Note: Zixia talked about how to correctly handle the relationship between learning and seeking to be an official. He said that officials should try to learn more knowledge so as to improve their governing capacities, and scholars who had learned well should try to secure official posts so as to serve the state, on condition that both had their spare energy. However, in today's China, it has become a common sense that one who studies excellently can and must become an official, thus officialdom seems to have become the only way out for excellent students. That is not what Zixia originally meant.

【今译】

子夏说："做官还有余力的人可以去学习; 学习有余力的人可以去做官。"

【注释】

1. 仕：当官。
2. 优：优闲，有余力。不可理解为"优秀"。

【解读】

子夏谈到如何正确处理读书学习和做官的关系。他说，官员们应该努力学习更多的知识，以提高他们的执政能力，而学者们应该争取获得官职，以服务国家，条件是两者都有多余的精力。然而，在后世，读书优秀的人可以而且必须当官已经成为一个共识，因此官场似乎已经成为优秀学生的唯一出路。这不是子夏最初的意思。

【句例】

1. 坚持学而优则仕，就能给国家提供人才。

If we keep to the notion that *a scholar with spare energy may seek to be an official*, we will be able to provide talents for the country.

2. 受学而优则仕错误观点的影响，他一读完大学就想做官。

Misled by the notion that *one who studies excellently must seek to be an official*, he sought to be an official soon after graduation from the university.

147 血气方刚

full of sap (vitality)
energetic
血气正旺
精力旺盛的

【出处】

孔子曰："君子有三戒：少之时，血气未定，戒之在色；及其壮也，血气方刚，戒之在斗；及其老也，血气既衰，戒之在得。"（论语 16.7）

Confucius said, "A man should guard against these three bad habits: in teenage years when immature, he should guard against carnal desire; in prime years when full of sap, he should guard against rivalry; in old age when physically decayed, he should guard against greed."

Note: Confucius pointed out that it was important to guard against different misdoings in a person's different life stages. He believed that a young man full of vitality was apt to be tempted by carnal lusts, and wanted them to take it as a warning. Today, "full of sap" has become a commendatory term specially used to describe a person who is full of vitality.

【今译】

孔子说："君子有三种事情应引以为戒：年少的时候，血气还不成熟，要戒除对女色的迷恋；到了盛年，血气正旺，要戒除争强好斗；到了老年，血气已经衰弱了，要戒除贪欲。"

【注释】

1. 戒：必须警惕而不能做的事。
2. 刚：旺盛。

【解读】

孔子指出，一个人在不同的人生阶段防范不同的错误是很重要的。他认为血气方刚的年轻人容易受到色情的诱惑，并要他们引以为戒。如今，"血气方刚"已经成为一个专门用来形容人充满活力的褒义词。

【句例】

1. 那些人血气方刚，风华正茂，是开发大西北的主力军。

Those people were *full of sap* in their prime years, and formed the main force for the development of the northwest area.

2. 几个血气方刚的青年办起了这个公司，为中欧间货物运输注入了又一股新的力量。

Several *energetic* young people set up this company, which has injected a new force into the transportation of goods between China and Europe.

148　学无常师

to learn without a regular teacher
求学没有固定的老师

【出处】

子贡曰：“夫子焉不学？而亦何常师之有？”（论语 19.22）

Zigong said, "Where could our master go without an opportunity of learning? And what need is there for him to have a regular teacher?"

Note: Zigong pointed out that the source of Confucius' learning was the doctrines of the great sages before him, like King Wen and King Wu of the Western Zhou Dynasty. Confucius, who lived in the Eastern Zhou Dynasty, could still learn from anybody who knew about the doctrines of King Wen and King Wu. He had no regular teachers and did not feel ashamed to learn from those who were inferior to him. This had contributed a lot to the breadth of his knowledge.

【今译】

子贡说：“我们老师哪儿学不到，何必一定要有固定的老师呢？”

【注释】

1. 夫子：子贡对孔子的尊称，相当于“我们的老师”。

2. 焉不学：哪儿学不到呢，意为随时随地可以学到知识。

【解读】

子贡指出，孔子的学识源自于先贤的学说，如西周的文王和武王。生活在东周的孔子仍然可以向任何了解文王和武王学说的人学习。他学无常师、不耻下问，这是他学识广博的原因。

【句例】

1. 这位画家的油画可谓出类拔萃。问他向谁学的，他说他学无常师。

It can be said the painter excelled in oil painting. When asked from whom he learned the skill, he said he *learned without a regular teacher.*

2. 那位作家年轻时学无常师，所以他糅合了多种不同的写作风格。

When he was young the writer *learned without a regular teacher*, so his writing style was a complex brew of many different sorts.

149　循循善诱

to guide somebody skillfully step by step
good at leading somebody gradually through a process
善于一步一步地诱导或引领

【出处】

颜渊喟然叹曰："夫子循循然善诱人，博我以文，约我以礼。"（论语 9.11）

Yan Yuan said with a deep sigh, "The Master skillfully guides us step by step. He broadens my learning, and regulates me with the rules of propriety."

Note: Yan Yuan, Confucius' best disciple, highly praised Confucius for guiding and instructing him in his academic studies and regulating him with the rules of propriety (the topmost code of conduct).

【今译】

颜渊感慨地说："老师善于一步一步地诱导我，用各种典籍来丰富我的知识，又用礼来约束我的言行。"

【注释】

1. 喟然：叹息的样子。

2. 循循然善诱人：善于有次序地引导人。循循然，有次序地。

【解读】

孔子最好的弟子颜渊高度赞扬孔子在学术研究上对他的引领和指导，并用礼仪规则（最高的行为准则）来规范他。

【句例】

1. 这位女教师对我们循循善诱，很快消除了我们初学荷兰语的恐惧。

This woman teacher *guided us skillfully step by step* in our first days of Dutch learning, and soon removed our fear of it.

2. 当时我学习基础差，正需要有个循循善诱的好老师。

I was poor in study at that time, and I did need a teacher who was *good at leading me gradually through my learning process*.

150 言必信，行必果

true to every word and stoutly seek a result in every action
说话一定要讲信用，行动一定要有结果

【出处】

子曰："言必信，行必果，硁硁然小人哉！抑亦可以为次矣。"（论语 13.20）

"Those who are true to every word and stoutly seek a result in every action are rigid petty fellows," the Master continued. "Still, they may be ranked next."

Note: Confucius tried to grade scholars in his time. According to him, the highest grade of scholars should be those who could accomplish something great for the state. And those who did less important things would belong to the lower grades. Confucius also put forth a very important principle: A great personage does not need to keep his promise if it is not based on just grounds. Today, however, keeping one's word is considered as a very important moral character.

【今译】

孔子说："说话一定要讲信用，行动一定要有结果，那是不问是非、固执浅薄的一般人啊。但也可以说是再次一等的士了。"

【注释】

1. 行必果：（1）行为必定果断。（2）所行必求有结果。今从后说。

2. 硁硁然小人：固执浅薄的一般人。指那些过于坚持小节而忽视大局的人。

【解读】

春秋时期，士作为治国的辅助力量已经崛起。孔子把士的表现的高低分为几个不同层次。最高的是属于治国平天下的层次；其次为以"孝悌"见称，属于齐家的层次。对于"言必信行必果"的士，孔子认为对于治理天下国家还不是大利，所以固守诺言的士被他贬低为"固执浅薄的一般人"，不过孔子还是承认他们属于士的范畴，只是等级略差一些罢了。一百多年后的孟子把"义"

当成言行的准则，凡事合乎公平、正义才去做，不然则诺言可不兑现。但在普通人的一般交往中，"言必信行必果"被看成是非常重要的为人的品德。

【句例】

1. 孟子说："大人者，言不必信，行不必果，惟义所在。"这是说只有理由正当我们才须要履行诺言。（原用法）

Mencius said, "Those in superior positions may not necessarily *be true to every word or stoutly seek a result of every action*; they base their choices only on justice." This means that we only need to fulfill a promise on just grounds.

2. 言必信，行必果，这是我们做人的基本要求。（现代用法）

It is a basic requirement for us to *be true to every word and seek a result of every action*.

151 言必有中

When he speaks, he is sure to hit the point.
When he says something, he is sure to hit the mark.
一开口就一定说到要害上。

【出处】

鲁人为长府。闵子骞曰："仍旧贯，如之何？何必改作？"子曰："夫人不言，言必有中。"（论语 11.14）

When the authority of Lu was to have the Treasury Mansion rebuilt, Min Ziqian said, "How about keeping it what it is? Why rebuild it?" Hearing that, the Master said, "This man seldom speaks, but once he speaks, he is sure to hit the point."

Note: The state ruler of Lu was planning to rebuild the Treasury Mansion. Well aware that the rebuilding would cause trouble, Min Ziqian wisely advised him not to rebuild it. Confucius agreed with him and said that what he said hit the nail on the head.

【今译】

鲁国打算翻修长府。闵子骞说："保持老样子，怎么样？何必改建呢？"孔子道："这个人平日不大开口，一开口就说到要害。"

【注释】

1. 为长府：改建长府。长府，鲁国府库名。
2. 仍旧贯：沿袭老样子。旧贯，旧例。
3. 言必有中：说话一定击中要害。

【解读】

此段话记孔子借赞扬闵子骞说话中肯表达他不赞成改建长府的意见。当时的季氏家族专横跋扈，架空鲁君，故鲁昭公与之矛盾相当激烈，而长府在这种对立中对双方均有战术意义。改建工作既加剧君臣矛盾，又劳民伤财，所以闵子骞婉言讽劝。孔子同样看出其中的隐患，故极力赞赏闵子骞的意见，说他的话正中要害。

【句例】

1. 总经理对所有细节往往都有深入仔细的研究，难怪他分析问题时每每言必有中。

The general manager will have a thorough study of all details. It's no wonder that he is *sure to hit the point* when he analyzes a problem.

2. 开会时他很少发表意见，但偶尔讲一两句，则言必有中。

He seldom spoke at a meeting, but when he did say something once in a while, he was *sure to hit the mark*.

152 言不及义

to talk about nothing serious
do not talk about justice (wrong!)
不讲正经事
不讲合乎义的事（错！）

【出处】

子曰："群居终日，言不及义，好行小慧，难矣哉！"（论语 15.17）

The Master said, "There are people who mingle with each other all day without talking about anything serious, but just love to show off their minor wisdom. Such people are really a hard case!"

Note: Confucius sharply criticized those who loved to show off their smartness in trivial matters without bothering to say or do anything meaningful.

【今译】

孔子说："整天聚在一块，从来不讲正经事，专好卖弄小聪明，这种人真是不可救药啊！"

【注释】

1. 言不及义：所说没有正经事。义，古时指合宜之事，即该做之事。

2. 小慧：小聪明。

【解读】

孔子严厉批评一些人喜欢在琐事上炫耀自己的小聪明而懒得说或做正经事。他告诫人们聚集在一起要讲正经话、做正经事，不要成天蜚短流长，讲些不着边际的话。

【句例】

1. 他这个人不读书、不看报，话很多，却言不及义，成天无所事事混过日子。

He won't read books or newspapers. He *talks* too much but it is *about nothing seri*ous. He idles around all day and accomplishes nothing.

2. 这群人倒是爱聊天，可惜不学无术，所以从来都是言不及义。

This group of people are fond of chatting, but unfortunately they are ignorant and refuse to learn, so they have *never talk about anything serious*. (It is wrong to say it like this: so they have *never talk about justice*.)

153 言而有信

to be faithful in word
to be as good as one's word
说话靠得住，有信用

【出处】

子夏曰："贤贤易色；事父母能竭其力；事君，能致其身；与朋友交，言而有信。虽曰未学，吾必谓之学矣。"（论语 1.7）

Zixia said, "If a man values the virtuous more than he does a beauty, if he does his utmost in serving his parents, if he can dedicate his life to serving his prince, if he is faithful in word among friends, I certainly consider him a good learner, though others might think otherwise."

Note: Zixia pointed out here that one should be true to his word in associating with others. In chapter 13.20 of the *Analects of Confucius* (see 150), Confucius said one should not necessarily be faithful in word. He was right to say that people in high positions didn't have to keep their word when their promises didn't accord with justice. However, in ordinary people's interactions, "keeping promises" is regarded as a very important moral character, so there is no contradiction between what Zixia said here and what Confucius said in that chapter.

【今译】

子夏说："一个人能够尊重贤明的人而不看重女色；侍奉父母能尽心竭力；服事君主能不惜献身；同朋友交往，说话算数守信用。这样的人，尽管有人说他没有学习过，我一定说他已经学习过了。"

【注释】

1. 贤贤易色：尊重贤明之人，看轻女色。第一个"贤"为动词，意即"尊重"，第二个"贤"为名词，即"贤人"。易，轻视、不看重的意思。

【解读】

孔子在《论语》13.20 章（见 150 条）讲到"言必信，行必果，硁硁然小人哉！"那说的是身居高位的人在不符合公理的情况下说话不一定要算数，是对的。但在普通人的一般交往中，"言必信行必果"被看成是非常重要的为人品德，所以这里子夏说的和该章孔子说的并没有矛盾。

【句例】

1. 只有做到言而有信，人家才愿意与你交往和合作。

People will be willing to communicate and cooperate with you only when you are *faithful in word*.

2. 他言而有信，九点钟冒着大雨准时出现了。

He was *as good as his word* and turned up at nine despite the heavy rain.

154　用行舍藏

Once used, take action; when discarded, live in seclusion.
to take action when used, and withdraw otherwise
得到任用就出来做事（或当官），得不到任用就隐退

【出处】

子谓颜渊曰："用之则行，舍之则藏，惟我与尔有是夫！"（论语 7.11）（注：请参阅 004 暴虎冯河，此句在该文之前。）

The Master said to Yan Yuan, "Once I am used, I'll take action; when I am discarded, I'll live in seclusion. Maybe it is only you and me who can make it!"

Note: Yan Yuan was a cautious and rational student, so Confucius loved to discuss with him about how to choose the best opportunity to work for the state and in what situation could he choose to withdraw from office.

【今译】

孔子对颜渊说："如果用我，我就行动起来；如果不用我，我就潜身隐退，能做到这样的，恐怕只有我和你啊！"

【注释】

1. 用之则行：指一个人若能为时所用，则出来做官，为国为民担当重任。

2. 舍之则藏：指一个人若不被任用，就不露锋芒，甚至隐居。舍，舍弃，不用，不被所用。藏，隐藏，隐居。

【解读】

颜渊是一个谨慎而理性的学生，因此孔子喜欢与他讨论如何选择为国家工作的最佳机会以及在什么情况下可以选择离职隐退。

【句例】

1. 用行舍藏，这是孔子决定是否参与救世的原则。但事实表明，他从未放弃希望和行动。

Once he was used, he would take action; when he was discarded, he would live in seclusion. This is the principle on which Confucius decided whether or not to help save the chaotic world. But the fact showed that he never give up hope or action.

2. 用行舍藏，这我知道，所以既然贵公司不用我，那我当然不会恋栈了。

I know I should *take action when used, and withdraw otherwise*, so since your company will not use me, I won't be reluctant to leave.

155 乐山乐水

to find pleasure in mountains and waters
to love mountains and rivers
喜爱山水

【出处】

子曰："知者乐水，仁者乐山；知者动，仁者静；知者乐，仁者寿。"（论语 6.23）

The Master said, "The wise find pleasure in waters while the virtuous take delight in mountains. The wise are active, the virtuous tranquil. The wise are happy, the virtuous longevous. "

Note: Confucius pointed out that the wise and the virtuous people love mountains and rivers. They love nature and enjoy happy and peaceful lives.

【今译】

孔子说："聪明人喜爱水，有仁德的人喜爱山；聪明人活动，仁德者沉静。聪明人快乐，有仁德的人长寿。"

【注释】

1. 知者：智者，聪明人。

2. 乐：以……为乐，动词，古音同"药"，喜爱的意思。

【解读】

孔子指出，智者和仁者热爱山水。他们热爱大自然，享受快乐和平静的生活。

【句例】

1. 如今，乐山乐水的人越来越多。虽然他们不是孔子说的仁者和智者，但懂得欣赏大自然的美。

Nowadays, more and more people *find pleasure in mountains and waters*. They are not virtuous or wise people as is defined by Confucius, but they are good at enjoying the beauty of nature.

2. 这群乐山乐水的退休老人几乎走遍了这一带所有的山村。

These retired old people *love mountains and rivers*. They have toured almost all the mountain villagers in this area.

156　一匡天下

to bring the kingdom to normal by rectifying it
to reunify the country
匡正（周）王国使之恢复正常秩序
统一天下

【出处】

子曰："管仲相桓公，霸诸侯，一匡天下，民到于今受其赐。(论语 14.17)
The Master said, "When Guan Zhong was prime minister, he helped Prince Huan to seek hegemony over all the states, and bring the kingdom to normal by rectifying it. Down to the present day the people are still enjoying the benefits he brought about.

Note: Prince Huan of the State of Qi appointed Guan Zhong as the Prime Minister. From then on, Guan Zhong began to help the prince to seek hegemony and achieved the goal of enriching the state and strengthening its military power. Guan Zhong persuaded Prince Huan to adopt the policy of "revering the king and resisting the outlying tribes", and controlled the entire kingdom in the name of the King of Zhou, which reduced the wars and killing between the princely states at that time and formed a seemingly unified situation in the Eastern Zhou Dynasty.

【今译】

孔子说："管仲辅佐桓公，称霸诸侯，匡正了天下，恢复正常秩序，老百姓到了今天还享受到他的好处。"

【注释】

1. 相：帮助，辅助，此处指当国相，即相当于后世的宰相。

2. 一匡天下：一指统一；匡指匡正；天下指当时的东周王朝。管仲助齐桓公称霸后，原来群龙无首的东周王朝的各诸侯国行动相对比较一致，争战杀伐的事也减少了。

【解读】

桓公任命管仲为相，从此开始了富国强兵的争霸历程。管仲说服桓公采用

"尊王攘夷"的政策，以周天子号令天下，扭转了当时诸侯国相互争战杀伐的局面，为东周王朝形成了表面上的统一局面。

【句例】

1. 在管仲辅助下，齐桓公称霸诸侯，一匡天下。

With the help of Guan Zhong, Prince Huan of the State of Qi gained hegemony over all the states, and *brought the kingdom to normal by rectifying it*.

2. 那个军事头目妄想借助武力一匡天下，结果当然是身败名裂了。

The military chief dreamed of *reunifying the country* by force, only to be utterly defeated and discredited.

157 以人废言 以言举人

to reject a good saying simply because of its speaker
(who is lower in position or has mistakes)
to favor or promote a man only because of his good words
因为一个人（地位低或犯错误）而抹杀他讲得好的话
因为一个人话说得好而看重、提拔他

【出处】

子曰："君子不以言举人，不以人废言。"（论语 15.23）

The Master said, "A superior man never favors a man only because of his good words, nor does he reject a good saying simply because of its speaker."

Note: Confucius warned that it was not right to judge a person simply by his good sayings or reject the good sayings of a person simply because he was lower in position or had mistakes.

【今译】

孔子说："君子不因一个人说的话好而推举他，也不因为一个人不好而抹杀他讲的正确的话。"

【注释】

1. 以言举人：仅仅因为某人话说得好而推举甚至重用他。

2. 以人废言：仅仅因为某人地位低或犯错误而抹杀他讲得好的话。

【解读】

此句讲君子的待人处世之道。一个人话讲得好，他的品质和能力不一定就好。听了他的话，还要看他的为人本质和实际行动，才能决定能否推举、重用他。同样地，一个人虽然有缺点错误，或者地位低下，但如果他的话讲得好，是有益的建言，照样可以采用。

【句例】

1. 他说的听起来不错，但我还得深入了解他。我不想以言举人。

What he said sounds fine, but I must get to know him better. I don't want to *favor a man only because of his good words*.

2. 此人的这句名言虽好但现在已经没人用了，因为他被定性为坏人。由此可见，以人废言如今还很常见。

This man's well-known saying is good but no longer quoted now, because he is labeled as a villian. It can be seen that nowadays it is common to *reject a good saying simply because of its speaker*.

158 一言兴邦 一言丧邦

A word may help boost a state.
A word may ruin a state.
一句话就可以使国家兴盛。
一句话就可以使国家衰败。

【出处】

定公问:"一言而可以兴邦,有诸?"孔子对曰:"言不可以若是,其几也。人之言曰:'为君难,为臣不易。'如知为君之难也,不几乎一言而兴邦乎?"(论语 13.15)

Prince Ding asked Confucius, "Is there such a word as may help boost a state?"

"A word cannot be as powerful as that," said the Master, "but it can be close to that.

"There is a saying that goes, 'To be the ruler is hard work; to be an official is not an easy job.' If a prince knows about the difficulty, isn't it almost true that a word may help boost a state?"

Note: According to Confucius, a state ruler should be very cautious about his words as they might affect the state governance greatly. A correct way of his might help boost his state, and a wrong word might cause him to lose his state.

【今译】

鲁定公问:"一句话就可以使国家兴盛,有这么回事吗?"孔子答道:"一句话不可能有像你所说的(有那么大的威力),但有时可能近乎如此。有人说:'做君难,做臣不易。'如果知道了做君主的难处,这不近乎一句话可以使国家兴盛吗?"

【注释】

1. 邦:国,即诸侯国。

2. 几:接近,差不多。

【解读】

按孔子的说法，国君应该对自己的言论非常谨慎，因为他的言论可能会对国家治理产生很大影响。他的一句正确的话可能有助于兴邦，而一句错误的话可能会导致他丧邦。

【句例】

1. 他的战略决策给这个国家带来了巨大的发展，正所谓一言兴邦啊！

His strategic decision has brought about great development in this country. This is what we call "*a word may help boost a state*"!

2. 一言可以兴邦，一言可以丧邦，大人物说话不得不谨慎啊。

A word may help boost a state; *a word may ruin a state*. Big shots have to be cautious in word.

159 一言以蔽之

to sum up in just one line（originally）
in a word, in short（today's usage）
用一句诗句来概括（原意）
简而言之（今用）

【出处】

子曰："诗三百，一言以蔽之，曰：'思无邪'。"（论语 2.2）

The Master said, "The *Book of Poetry* with all its three hundred poems may be summed up in a just one line: 'With pure thoughts'."

Note: Confucius believed that the nature of the *Book of Poetry* could be summarized in one sentence, that is, with pure thoughts, which means that the ideas expressed in its poems are pure and innocent, all in line with the moral principles recognized by the society at that time. Many poems denouncing the darkness of the society and expressing the love between men and women could be regarded as the proper expression of human feelings rather than evil thoughts.

【今译】

孔子说："《诗》三百篇，可以用一句话来概括，就是'思想纯正'。"

【注释】

1. 诗三百：《诗》的另一称呼。《诗》是中国古代第一部诗歌总集，收入自西周初年至春秋中叶五百多年的诗歌 305 篇，西汉时被尊为儒家经典，始称《诗经》。

2. 一言：（原文）一句诗句，a line of poem.（今意）一句话，a word.

3. 蔽：概括。

4. 思无邪：《诗经·鲁颂·駉》一句，原指马儿不斜跑。"思"原为语首词，无义，此处引用时作"思想"解；无邪亦作"纯正"解。

【解读】

　　孔子认为用一句话就可以概括《诗》的性质，那就是：思无邪，意思是，《诗》中的作品所表达的思想纯正无邪，全部符合于当时社会公认的道德原则。许多斥责统治黑暗、表现男女爱情的诗歌，都可以看成是人的感情的正当流露，而不能看成诗人的邪念。

【句例】

　　1. 一言以蔽之，问题的症结在于思想方法的陈旧。

In a word, the crux of the problem lies in the obsolescent ways of thinking.

　　2. 对于这类项目，我不赞成对外融资。一言以蔽之，此路不通。

As for this type of project, I am not in favor of foreign capital financing for it. *In short,* this is the dead end.

160　一以贯之

one principle that runs all through a doctrine
constant, constantly
用一个总体原则贯通事情的始末
一贯的，一贯地

【出处】

子曰："参乎，吾道一以贯之。"曾子曰："唯。"子出，门人问曰："何谓也？"曾子曰："夫子之道，忠恕而已矣。"（论语 4.15）

The Master said, "Oh, Shen, there is one principle that runs all through my doctrines." "Yes," replied Zengzi. When the Master went out, other disciples asked Zengzi, "What did the Master mean?" "He was telling me about his doctrines, which just boil down to faithfulness and reciprocity," replied Zengzi.

Note: Zeng Shen (Zengzi) said that "faithfulness" and "reciprocity" was the overall principle that ran through all his teacher's doctrines. "Faithfulness" means to work dedicatedly for the good of others; "reciprocity" means to think in other people's place for their good.

【今译】

孔子说："参啊，我的学说是由一个总体原则贯彻始终的。"曾子说："是的。"孔子出去之后，有个同学问曾子："老师说的是什么意思啊？"曾子说："老师说的原则，就是忠恕而已。"

【注释】

1. 参：即曾参，孔子重要弟子，敬称曾子。

2. 一以贯之：以一个总体原则贯彻始终。曾子认为这个总体原则就是"忠恕"。

3. 忠恕：忠，指对人尽心尽力；恕，指设身处地为他人着想，己所不欲勿施于人。

【解读】

曾参（曾子）说，"忠"和"恕"是贯穿孔子所有学说的总体原则。"忠"指尽心尽力为他人做事；"恕"指站在他人的位置替他人着想，己所不欲勿施于人。

【句例】

1. 本公司注重产品质量，这是我们生产过程中一以贯之的原则。

We attach importance to the quality of our company's products, and this has been our principle *that runs through the process of* our production.

2. 精益求精是我们一以贯之的信念。

Striving for excellence is our *constant* belief.

161　以德报怨　以直报怨

to return good for evil　to return justice for evil

【出处】

或曰："以德报怨，何如？"子曰："何以报德？以直报怨，以德报德。"（论语 14.34）

Someone asked Confucius, "What do you think of returning good for evil?"

"If so, with what do you return for good?" said Confucius, "Return justice for evil and return good for good."

Note: Confucius put forth his important principle on how to treat others in return for their favor or malice. A so-called Confucius maxim is often quoted: "Return good for evil." Now we know that is not true. According to Confucius, we should do the right thing to deal with the bad things that others have done to us.

【今译】

有人说："用恩德来回报仇怨，怎么样？"孔子说："那样的话，用什么来回报恩德呢？应该是用公正来回报仇怨，用恩德来回报恩德。"

【注释】

1. 以德报怨：用恩德来回报仇怨。怨，指因别人的恶行和加害而结下的仇怨。

2. 以直报怨：用公正合理的态度来回应别人的仇怨。也就是面对别人的恶意加害，采取符合公平正义的方法予以应对或还击。

【解读】

孔子纠正别人对他一条言论的误解。常听人说，"孔子教导我们要以德报怨"，其实孔子并没有说过这样的话。"以德报怨"出自老子《道德经》，说的是以恩德来化解怨恨。孔子主张以德报德，但不赞成以德报怨，而主张"以直报怨"，即按社会公义去处理仇怨。

【句例】

1. 车祸受害者以德报怨，主动减轻了肇事者的赔偿。

The victim of the car accident *returned good for evil*, and offered to take less compensation from the perpetrator.

2. 这事我只能以直报怨，一条条反驳他的诽谤。

For this I could only *return justice for evil*, and refuted every one of his slanders.

162 以文会友

to gather friends on literary grounds
通过文章学问来结交朋友

【出处】

曾子曰："君子以文会友，以友辅仁。"（论语 12.24）

Zengzi said, "A superior man gathers friends on literary grounds, and fosters his own morality with the help of such friends."

Note: Zengzi pointed out that true good friends were those who could gather together to study ancient classics and exchange ideas so that both sides could make progress in literary talent and morality.

【今译】

曾子说："君子以文章学问来结交朋友，依靠朋友帮助自己培养仁德。"

【注释】

1. 以文会友：指友好相处，一起学习，共同探讨，互相砥砺。文，这里指对古代经典的研习和文章的写作。

【解读】

曾子指出，真正的好朋友是那些可以聚集在一起研究古代经典和交流思想的人，这样双方可以在文学才华和道德方面取得进步。

【句例】

1. 此次论坛的宗旨是以文会友，希望更多的同好能踊跃参加。

The purpose of this forum is to *gather friends on literary grounds*, and we hope that more literary lovers will join us actively.

2. 那是一次以文会友的盛会，几乎全城的有名诗人都与会共襄盛举。

That was a great meeting to *gather friends on literay grounds* and almost all noted poets in town participated to mark the event.

163　有教无类

Education for all regardless of learners' backgrounds.
对谁都要进行教育，不要区别对待不同类别的对象。

【出处】

子曰："有教无类。"（论语 15.39）

The Master said, "Let there be education for all regardless of learners' backgrounds."

Note: Confucius declared that education should be open to all without any discrimination against any individual. Confucius was the greatest educationist in ancient China. He did have disciples from all backgrounds.

【今译】

孔子说："对谁都要进行教育，不要区别对待不同类别的对象。"

【注释】

1. 无类：不分类。孔子吸收学生不问背景，为平民子弟入学创造了最基本的条件。

【解读】

有教无类是孔子的伟大的教育思想。春秋时期，教育已不再是贵族的专利。孔子所做的，就是把贵族文化推及平民。而要做到这一点，首先要求学生来源越广越好。孔子吸收学生，不看背景，无论尊卑、贫富、智愚、贤贱都能来者不拒。他的学生除两位出身贵族外，其余为平民、贫民、破落贵族、商人、奴隶等，其中还有品行不端者，但最终大都学有所成，有些甚至成了社会显达之士，这是孔子被称为中国古代最伟大的平民教育家的原因之一。"有教无类"（Education for all）已经成为联合国教科文组织的口号。

【句例】

1. 有教无类是极难追求的目标。在这方面，孔子进行了史上最成功的实践。

Education for all regardless of learners' backgrounds is a most difficult goal to pursue. In this regard, Confucius undertook the most successful practice in history.

2. "有教无类运动"（EFA）是联合国教科文组织领导下的全球性运动，旨在满足全球儿童、青年和成年人的教育需求。（摘自维基百科）

Education For All (EFA) is a global movement led by UNESCO (United Nation Educational, Scientific and Cultural Organization), aiming to meet the learning needs of all children, youth and adults. (from Wikipedia)

164　愚不可及

stupidity that is beyond others' reach (originally)
extremely stupid (variant today)
大智若愚，别人学不来（原意）
极端愚蠢（今解）

【出处】

子曰："宁武子，邦有道则知，邦无道则愚，其知可及也，其愚不可及也。"（论语 5.21）

The Master said, "This is Ningwuzi: when good government prevailed in the state, he showed his wisdom. When ill government prevailed in the state, he appeared stupid. His wisdom is within others' reach, his stupidity beyond others' reach."

Note: Ningwuzi was a minister of the State of Wei. When the state was well run, he showed his wisdom. When the state was in great disorder, he endured humiliation quietly, doing things that others might consider to be stupid, and managed to keep the state from falling apart. His stupidity was in fact great wisdom that saved his state from catastrophe, and it was beyond the reach of others.

【今译】

孔子说："宁武子这个人，当国家政治清明时，他就显得聪明；当国家政局混乱时，他就装傻。他的这种聪明是别人所能及的，他的大智若愚是别人所不能及的。"

【注释】

1. 宁武子：姓宁名俞，卫国大夫，"武"是他的谥号。

2. 原句中的两个"知"字都同"智"。

3. 愚不可及：装糊涂的策略别人难以学到。今意，愚蠢到极点。

【解读】

宁武子是卫国大臣。国家政治清明时，他展现智慧为国效力。国家政局混乱时，他默默忍受屈辱，做着别人可能认为愚蠢的事情，以设法使国家免于分崩离析。他的愚蠢实际上是一种大智慧，使他的国家免于灾难，这是其他人无法企及的。

【句例】

1. 他放弃百万年薪而到荒原造林。许多人说他愚，我则慨叹其愚不可及，因为没人能达到他的思想境界。

He gave up his million-dollar annual salary and went to reforest a wasteland. Many people say he is stupid, but I would rather say *his stupidity is beyond other people's reach,* for no one else can reach that realm of thought of his.

2. 以健康换金钱实在是愚不可及。

It is *extremely stupid* to earn money at the expense of health.

165 欲罢不能

could hardly stop
unwilling to give up
想停下来都不可能
难以舍弃

【出处】

颜渊曰："夫子循循然善诱人，博我以文，约我以礼，欲罢不能。即竭吾才，如有所立卓尔。虽欲从之，末由也已。"（论语 9.11）

Yan Yuan said, "The Master skillfully guides us step by step. He broadens my learning, and regulates me with the rules of propriety, so that I could hardly stop my learning. Having exerted all my abilities, I find something lofty standing right up before me. I try to follow it, but find no way to it."

Note: Yan Yuan, Confucius' best disciple, highly praised Confucius for guiding and instructing him in his academic studies and regulating him with the rules of propriety. Yan Yuan said that Confucius' doctrine was so hard for him but he would not stop learning it.

【今译】

颜渊说："老师善于一步一步地诱导我，用各种典籍来丰富我的知识，又用礼来约束我的言行，使我想停止学习都不可能。我已经用尽了我的才智，但好像有一个十分高大的东西立在我前面。虽然我想要追随它，却找不到途径。"

【注释】

1. 卓尔：高大、超群的样子。
2. 末由：没有办法。末，无、没有。由，途径，路径。

【解读】

孔子最好的弟子颜渊（颜回）高度赞扬孔子在学术上对他的引领和指导，并用礼来规范他。颜回说孔子的学说对他来说太难了，但他同时表示，不管有多难，他都不会停止学习。

【句例】

1. 围棋学到这个阶段，孩子们感觉已经是欲罢不能了。

Having reached this stage of Go learning, the children have come to feel that they *can hardly stop* now.

2. 无人机研究如此有趣，换谁都欲罢不能。

The drone research is so interesting that *none* of them, no matter who he is, *would be unwilling to give it up.*

166 欲速则不达

More haste, less speed.
Haste makes waste.
求快反而达不到目的。

【出处】

子曰："无欲速，无见小利。欲速则不达，见小利则大事不成。"（论语13.17）

The Master said, "Do not want things done hastily; do not covet petty gains. More haste, less speed. Coveting petty gains will fail great accomplishment."

Note: Confucius warned his disciple Zixia not to try to seek quick success or be covetous of small gains.

【今译】

孔子说："不要求快，不要贪求小利。求快反而达不到目的，贪求小利就做不成大事。"

【注释】

1. 欲速则不达：性急求快反而达不到目的。

【解读】

此句记孔子向子夏讲解为政的策略。孔子要求他的学生子夏从政不要急功近利，否则就无法达到目的；不要贪求小利，否则就做不成大事。

【句例】

1. 没有充分准备就不要急着行动。欲速则不达。
Don't take action hastily without full preparations. *More haste, less speed.*
2. 欲速则不达。这种全面开花的政策对典籍外译的发展没有任何积极作用。

Haste makes waste. Such a policy of full swing won't have any positive effect on the development of foreign language translations of Chinese classics.

167　怨天尤人　不怨天，不尤人

to blame either men or heaven　to make complaint
to blame neither men nor heaven　to make no complaint
埋怨天，责备人
不埋怨天，不责备人

【出处】

子曰："莫我知也夫！"子贡曰："何为其莫知子也？"子曰："不怨天，不尤人。下学而上达，知我者其天乎！"（论语 14.35）

The Master said, "Alas! There is no one who understands me!"

"Why do you say so?" asked Zigong.

"I blame neither heaven nor men. I learn earthly knowledge and understand the course of heaven. Maybe it is only heaven that understands me!" explained the Master.

Note: Confucius was disappointed that his doctrine was not used by state rulers. However, he did not blame anyone for his not being understood, for he believed that everything was determined by heaven.

【今译】

孔子说："没有人了解我啊！"子贡说："为什么说没有人了解您呢？"孔子说："我不埋怨天，也不责备人，我下学人事，上知天道，了解我的大概只有天吧！"

【注释】

1. 尤：责怪、怨恨。

2. 下学上达：学习人情事理，进而领悟天道。人们学习知识，总是从最基本和最现实的知识开始，这就是"下学"。这种积累多了，就会悟出一些高深的道理，包括对天道的领悟。这就是"上达"。

【解读】

孔子对他的学说没有被某个国君所采用感到失望。然而，他没有因为自己的不被理解而责怪任何人，因为他相信一切都是上天决定的。

【句例】

1. 跟你们这些人成天怨天尤人不同，他默默地应对各种危机。

Unlike you people who *blame either men or heaven (make complaint)* every day, he quietly copes with various crises.

2. 我们不怨天不尤人，而是承担起这件事的责任。

We blame neither men nor heaven (make no complaint about anything), but choose to take the responsibility for this matter.

168 择善而从 择其不善而改之

to pick another one's good merits and emulate them
to find others' demerits to amend one's own
选择好的学，按照好的做
找到别人缺点，改掉自己同样的缺点

【出处】

子曰："二人行，必有我师焉。择其善者而从之，其不善者而改之。"（论语 7.22）

The Master said, "In a party of three there must be one whom I can learn from. I will pick his good merits to emulate them, and find his demerits to amend mine."

Note: Confucius advocated learning from others. According to him, when others do good, we should learn from them and do good accordingly. And we should also learn from those who do wrong, with the purpose to check if we have made the same mistakes so that we can correct them accordingly. This is a highly conscious attitude toward learning.

【今译】

孔子说："三人同行，肯定有一个是值得我学习的。我选择他们的优点而加以仿效，并找出他们的缺点以改掉我身上类似的缺点。"

【注释】

1. 三人行：一行三人，借指不大的一群人。不是"三个人一起步行"。

2. 择其善者：选择他们好的方面。

【解读】

孔子提倡向别人学习。别人做得好的，就要学到来，化为自己的行动，这叫做择善而从。另一方面，孔子也提倡以不善者为师，即参照别人身上的不善而作自我检查，以便改掉自身类似的不善，这是一种高度自觉的学习态度。

【句例】

1. 我跟他关系不是很好。但既然他做得好，我也只好择善而从了。

I was not on good terms with him. But since he did well, I had no choice but to *pick his good merits to emulate them*.

2. 不要嫌弃行为不端的人，而应该择其不善而改之。

Don't despise people who behave improperly. Instead, you should *find their demerits to amend your own*.

169 战战兢兢

to be cautious with reverence and awe
to tremble with fear
诚惶诚恐、小心谨慎
怕得发抖

【出处】

曾子有疾，召门弟子曰："启予足！启予手！诗云：'战战兢兢，如临深渊，如履薄冰.' 而今而后，吾知免夫，小子！"（论语 8.3）

When Zengzi was very ill, he summoned his disciples to the bedside and said, "Uncover my feet! And my hands! The *Book of Poetry* says, 'Be cautious with reverence and awe, as if approaching an abyss, or treading on thin ice.' I know from now on it will save me from any body injury, my boys!"

Note: As he believed that keeping a sound body was the best filial piety to parents, Zengzi had been trying cautiously to avoid any body injure, and now before he died he had his disciples come to confirm that his body was all right so that he could die without any regret.

【今译】

曾子有病，把他的学生召集到身边来，说道："掀开被子看看我的脚！看看我的手！《诗》上说：'诚惶诚恐、小心谨慎，好像站在深渊旁边，好像踩在薄冰上面.' 从今以后，我知道我的身体是不再会受到毁伤了，弟子们！"

【注释】

1. 启：开启，掀开。曾子让弟子们掀开被子看自己的手脚。
2. 战战兢兢：因害怕而微微发抖，也形容小心谨慎的样子。
3. 免：指身体免于毁伤。

【解读】

曾子是春秋时有名的大孝子。孔子有"身体发肤受之父母，不敢毁伤"的教导，曾子记了一辈子，把不让身体发肤受损作为孝敬父母的重要内容之一，非常诚惶诚恐、小心谨慎地保护自己的身体。临终前，他召来自己的弟子，来到床边看他的身体，作"最后验收"，见证自己的身体发肤并无受到毁伤，以证明对得起生养自己的父母，好让自己死而无憾。

【句例】

1. 对待国务院新闻发言人的工作她是战战兢兢，所以从来没出过差错。

As a spokeswoman for the State Council, she was *cautious with reverence and awe*, so she never made a mistake.

2. 我站在老板面前，战战兢兢，像一个犯了严重刑事罪的人。

I stood before the boss *trembling with fear*, like a man who had made a severe criminal offence.

170 朝闻夕死

If told of the Truth in the morning, one would die
willingly even in the evening.
Upon hearing the Way in the morning, one could die content in the evening.
早晨求得了真理（道），哪怕晚上死去也心甘。

【出处】

子曰："朝闻道，夕死可矣。"（论语 4.8）

The Master said, "If I were told of the Truth in the morning, I could die willingly even in the evening."

Note: This shows that Confucius had a very strong desire to pursue the truth, and he believed that in pursuing the truth, it was never too late for one to gain it.

【今译】

孔子说："早晨求得了真理，就是当天晚上死去也心甘。"

【注释】

1. 道：具体来说是一种方法、道理、原则、主张、思想、理论等；从更高层面的意义来说，是指涵盖并指导上述具体内容的总的学说、主义、真理、规律等。

【解读】

此句显示孔子闻道不嫌迟的豁达胸怀。孔子一直寻求治国之道，虽然屡遭挫折而心志不移，所以才有那种求得了道死了也心甘的气魄。此句现在常用来形容对真理或某种信仰追求的决心和执着心态。

【句例】

1. 古人重求道，哪怕是朝闻夕死也心甘情愿。

The ancients valued the pursuing of the Way so much that *if they were told of the Way in the morning, they would die willingly even in the evening.*

2. 追求真理是一辈子最的大事，哪怕是朝闻夕死也值得。

Pursuing the Truth is the first important thing for all one's life, so it it worthwhile that one *could die content in the evening upon hearing the Truth in the morning.*

171 贞而不谅

to uphold justice, but do not necessarily keep faith on minor issues
to keep integrity but not keep word blindly
固守正道，而不拘泥于小信
守正而不盲目守信

【出处】

子曰："君子贞而不谅。"（论语 15.37）

The Master said, "A superior man upholds justice, but does not necessarily keep faith on minor issues."

Note: Confucius pointed out that those in higher positions should stick to great principles, but it was not always necessary to keep the promise they made on some minor issues, especially when it was not made on just grounds.

【今译】

孔子说："君子固守正道，而不拘泥于小信。"

【注释】

1. 贞：坚定不变，坚持原则不动摇。

2. 不谅：指在某些情况下"诺言不一定要兑现"。谅，守信用。

【解读】

孔子重视"信"的道德原则，但也指出，信必须以合乎道义为前提。他说的"不谅"，是指在与重大道义原则冲突的细节问题上说话可以不算数，也就是孟子说的"大人者，言不必信，行不必果，惟义所在"。人非圣贤，作出的承诺有时难免会违背道义，这种情况下如果还认定说了就要算数，再加上说话者是个掌管重要事务的官员，那就会给国家带来损失。

【句例】

1. 大人物贞而不谅，目的是为了国家的利益。

Great personages uphold justice, but do not necessarily keep faith on minor issues. They do so for the benefits of the country.

2. 他贞而不谅，并且不怕别人的非议。

He keeps integrity and does not keep his word blindly, and he is not afraid of criticism from others.

172 直道而行

to go on the right way
to act rightly
沿着正道走
行事正直

【出处】

子曰："吾之于人也，谁毁谁誉？如有所誉者，其有所试矣。斯民也，三代之所以直道而行也。"（论语 15.25）

The Master said, "With regard to others, who did I ever defame and who did I ever praise? If I did praise some, it was because they had proved to be good. And they were all people who helped the three dynasties to go on the right way."

Note: Confucius said he never debased or praised a person groundlessly, and that when he wanted to praise some people, he would check if they were worthy of his praise. In this way he did praise some sage kings or virtuous people of the previous dynasties. He believed that it was those people who helped push the previous dynasties to go on the right way.

【今译】

孔子说："我对于别人，诋毁过谁？赞誉过谁？如果确有所赞誉，那是因为他们是经过检验证明了的。正是凭借这样的人，夏、商、周三代得以沿正道发展。"

【注释】

1. 试：考察，检验。
2. 斯民：那些人，即夏商周三代的圣人贤人。
3. 三代：夏商周三个朝代的合称。这是孔子所向往的时代。
4. 所以：所凭借的。以，凭借。

【解读】

孔子说他从不毫无根据地贬低或赞扬一个人，当他想赞扬一些人时，他会检查他们是否值得他的赞扬。通过这种方式，他确实赞扬了夏商周三个朝代的一些贤明的国王或贤德的人。他认为正是这些人帮助推动前朝直道而行，也就是走上了正确的道路。

【句例】

1. 本地区的经济要能直道而行，就必须先排除错误思想的干扰。

If the economy of this region is to *go on the right way*, the interference of erroneous ideas should be ruled out first.

2. 他这人处事总是直道而行，从不走歪门邪道。

He always *acts rightly* in handling affairs, and will never resort to any crooked means.

173　知其不可而为之

to keep doing what one knows is impossible
not to give up though one knows he may not make it
明知做不到却还要去做

【出处】

子路宿于石门。晨门曰："奚自？"子路曰："自孔氏。"曰："是知其不可而为之者与？"（论语 15.25）

Zilu stopped over Gate Shimen for the night. The next morning the gatekeeper asked him, "Where do you come from?"

"From Mr. Kong," replied Zilu.

"Well," said the gatekeeper, "do you mean the one who keeps doing what he knows is impossible?"

Note: Confucius took it as his responsibility to help save the disordered kingdom and tried every possible means to put his doctrine into practice. Some people viewed him as one who stuck to his principle all his life and would never give up even when he knew it was impossible for him to achieve the goal.

【今译】

子路夜里投宿石门，看门的人问："从哪里来？"子路说："从孔子那里来。"看门的人说："是那个明知做不到却还要去做的人吗？"

【注释】

1. 石门：地名。鲁国都城的外门。

2. 晨门：早上看守城门的人。

【解读】

明知做不到却还要去做，这是当时一些隐士和普通人对孔子的看法，也是孔子生平的真实写照。孔子一生奔波于列国之间，宣传他的学说和治国理念，希望为哪位国君所用，以便恢复周礼，实行仁政，安定社会。在崇尚以武力争战的春秋末期，他的理念被认为迂阔不切实际，屡屡不得见用，但他一直没有放弃，这种为理想坚持奋斗不懈的精神曾经鼓励和影响过无数仁人志士。

【句例】

1. 最终成功的，往往是那些知其不可而为之的人。

Those who succeed eventually are usually men who *keep doing what they know is impossible*.

2. 他十几年如一日坚持翻译《诗经》，知其不可而为之，精神可嘉。

He persisted in translating the *Book of Poetry* for more than a decade. He was worth praising since he *never gave up though he knew he might not make it*.

174 志士仁人

men of ideal and moral integrity
有高尚志向和道德情操的人

【出处】

子曰："志士仁人，无求生以害仁，有杀身以成仁。"（论语 15.9）

The Master said, "A man of ideal and moral integrity should not seek to survive at the expense of morality, but should be ready to give up his life for a just cause."

Note: Confucius pointed out that a man of ideal and moral integrity should be prepared to give life for a just cause, and should not try to preserve life at the expense of justice.

【今译】

孔子说："志士仁人，不能牺牲仁德来保全性命，而是要牺牲性命来保全仁德。"

【注释】

1. 害仁：损害仁德，违背道德价值。

2. 杀身以成仁：为维护道德和正义而献身。

【解读】

孔子指出为人要有献身理想的愿望和勇气。他认为在关键时刻，一个人不能以牺牲道德价值为代价来苟全性命，而要能为维护道德和正义而献身。这已经成了古往今来无数仁人志士坚守的人生原则。

【句例】

1. 富民强国，这是古往今来无数志士仁人为之奋斗的目标。

To make the people rich and the country strong is the goal that countless *men of ideal and moral integrity* have been striving for from ancient times till this day.

2. 向敌人投降当然为所有志士仁人所不齿。

Surrendering to the enemy would certainly be despised by all *men of ideal and moral integrity*.

175　致远恐泥

A small skill might hinder a lofty target.
Small skills are not helpful to great undertakings.
小技艺有可能会妨碍大目标。
小技无补于大业。

【出处】

子夏曰："虽小道，必有可观者焉，致远恐泥，是以君子不为也。"（论语
19.4）

Zixia said, "Although some skills are minor ones, they are certainly useful, except that they might hinder a lofty target, so a superior man does not practice them."

Note: A superior man here refers to a person who occupies a higher leadership position. They shoulder great responsibilities so they must have the overall leadership ability of governing their state, and do not limit themselves to certain minor skills. If they indulge in some certain skills, it may hinder the realization of their lofty goals. So it can be said that small skills are not helpful to great undertakings.

【今译】

子夏说："虽然是一些小技艺，也必定有可取的地方，但有时恐怕会阻碍人们达到远大目标，所以君子不从事这些小事。"

【注释】

1. 小道：指农工商医卜之类的各种技能。
2. 致远：走得远，指达到远大目标。
3. 泥：阻滞，不通，妨碍。

【解读】

君子在这里指居于较高领导地位者。他们任重而道远，所以必须掌握"大道"，也就是治理家国的通盘领导才干，而不拘于一才一艺。假如耽于某一才

艺，恐怕会妨碍实现远大目标，可见小技无补于大业。

【句例】

1. 致远恐泥的一个典型的例子就是明朝皇帝明熹宗。他沉湎于木工制作，差点毁掉明王朝。

A small skill might hinder a lofty target. One typical example is related to Emperor Xizong of the Ming Dynasty. He indulged in carpentry and almost ruined the Empire of Ming.

2. 高层领导者应该记住致远恐泥的古训，将主要精力放在治国大方略上。

High-ranking leaders should remember the old adage that *small skills are not helpful to great undertakings*, and focus on the the great strategy of state administration.

176　知之为知之，不知为不知

When you know a thing, say that you know it, when you
do not know a thing, say that you do not know it.
Don't pretend to know what you don't understand.
知道就是知道，不知道就是不知道。
不要不懂装懂。

【出处】

子曰："由，诲女知之乎？知之为知之，不知为不知，是知也。"（论语 2.17）
The Master said, "You, do you know what I have taught you? When you know a thing, say that you know it; when you do not know a thing, say that you do not know it. It is wise doing so."

Note: Confucius required his disciple Zhong You (Zilu) to have a down-to-earth attitude in learning, and warned him not to pretend to know what he didn't know.

【今译】

孔子说："仲由，我教你的，你知道了吗？知道就是知道，不知道就是不知道，这就是智慧啊！"

【注释】

1. 由：即仲由，姓仲名由，字子路。

2. 知：前面的五个"知"都是"知道、了解、明白"的意思。最后一个"知"同"智"，即智慧，明智。

【解读】

孔子要求他的弟子仲由（子路）在学习上要有脚踏实地的态度，并告诫他不要不懂装懂。

【句例】

1. 知之为知之，不知为不知，说的是不要不懂装懂。

When you know a thing, say that you know it, when you do not know a thing, say that you do not know it. This means that you should not pretend to know what you don't understand.

2. 知之为知之，不知为不知，这是求取知识的一种脚踏实地的态度。

Don't pretend to know what you don't understand. This reflects a down-to-earth attitude in acquiring knowledge.

177 自经沟渎

to hang oneself in a small valley
to commit suicide in the wild
to die an unworthy death
在小山沟里上吊
在野外自杀
死得不值得

【出处】

子曰："微管仲，吾其被发左衽矣。岂若匹夫匹妇之为谅也，自经于沟渎而莫之知也。"（论语 14.17）

The Master said, "But for Guan Zhong, we might now be wearing our hair unbound with barbarian clothes on.

"How can you expect him to show minor fidelity (to his late master) like a common man or woman, and hang himself in a small valley without being known to any?"

Note: （the same as Notes of 090 and 091）

【今译】

孔子说："如果没有管仲，恐怕我们也要披散着头发，衣襟向左开了。哪能要求他像普通百姓那样信守小节（为他已故的主人殉节），在小山沟里上吊自杀而不能为世所知呀。"

【注释】

1. 自经：上吊自杀。
2. 沟渎：沟渠。渎（dú），小渠。

【解读】

（同 091 的【解读】）

【句例】

1. 我不想自经沟渎。我要活着跟恶势力作斗争。

I don't want to *hang myself in the wild*. I will live to fight against the evil forces.

2. 他自经沟渎以证清白，而不是与法律的不公进行抗争。

Instead of fighting against the injustice of law, he *committed suicide* to prove his innocence.

178　中道而废

to give up halfway
走到一半路就停下来
半途而废

【出处】

冉求曰："非不说子之道，力不足也。"子曰："力不足者，中道而废。今女画。"（论语 6.12）

Ran Qiu said, "It is not that I don't like your doctrines, but that I am not capable enough."

"The incapable may give up halfway only after they have tried. Now you have simply drawn a circle to confine yourself," the Master rebutted.

Note: Ran Qiu was then serving the Jisun Family whose chief was the prime minster of the State of Lu. He wanted to increase agricultural taxes for the Jisun's Family by changing the land rent system, and asked Confucius for advice on this matter. Confucius explicitly told him to reduce taxes. But Ran Qiu didn't want to listen to him. Instead, he said that he was not competent enough to learn. Confucius retorted that people with insufficient ability were at least willing to try, and stop halfway if they were really incapable, but Ran Qiu didn't even want to try. Confucius was so angry that he "incited" his other disciples to "beat the drum to attack him".

【今译】

冉求说："我不是不喜欢老师您的学说主张，而是我的能力不够呀。"孔子说："能力不够的人是干到半途才停下来，现在你是给自己画地自限。"

【注释】

1. 说：同"悦"，喜欢。
2. 中道而废：做到一半才停止。废，放弃，停止。
3. 女画：你画地自限，不愿跨出一步。

【解读】

冉求当时正在鲁国国相季孙家任职。他想利用改变田赋制度为季氏增加赋税，并为此事征求孔子意见。孔子明确告诉他要"敛从其薄"。但冉求不愿意听老师的告诫，还说自己能力不足，学不来。孔子反驳说，能力不足的人起码愿意试，试到一半不行才停下来，而冉求根本连试都不想试。对此孔子非常生气，甚至鼓动其他弟子"鸣鼓而攻之"。

【句例】

1. 值得做的事情就要坚持做到底。中道而废是一个人意志力不强的表现。

Something worthy to be done should be carried out to the end. It is a lack of willpower to *give up halfway*.

2. 好的领导者做事一贯有始有终，从来不中道而废。

A good leader will complete what he has started to do and never *give up halfway*.

179 中庸之道

the doctrine of the mean
the Golden Mean
the Principle of Impartiality
中庸之道

【出处】

子曰："中庸之为德也，其至矣乎！民鲜久矣。"（论语 6.29）

The Master said, "The Golden Mean as a great virtue must have reached its highest realm! But it hasn't been seen in the people for a long time."

Note: Confucius admired very much the doctrine of the mean. The doctrine of the mean is not eclecticism, let alone unprincipled mediocrity, but a kind of very high wisdom. The doctrine of the mean plays an even greater role in state administration and people's self-cultivation. It helps individuals or governments to avoid going to extremes when dealing with problems, so as to adopt the moderate methods to achieve the ideal results. However, Confucius pointed out that people at that time rarely practiced the doctrine of the mean, which brought about all kinds of riots, disputes and destruction.

【今译】

孔子说："中庸作为一种道德，该是最高的了吧！人们缺少这种道德已经很久了。"

【注释】

1. 中庸：即中庸之道。中庸之道是孔子重要思想之一，也是儒家最高德行标准。力行中庸，就是遇事处事善于权衡各种可能，不走极端，"执两用中"、"无过无不及"，寻求最佳解决办法。

2. 鲜：少。

【解读】

孔子对中庸推崇备至。中庸之道不是折衷主义，更不是不讲原则的庸人主义，而是一种极高的智慧。在治理国家和修身养性方面，中庸之道的作用就更大了。它能让个人或政府在处理问题时避免走极端，从而采取最为适中的方法以达到最理想的效果。但孔子在文中指出，当时的人很少能实行中庸之道，代之而起的是各种暴乱、纷争和破坏。

【句例】

1. 中庸之道不是折中主义哲学，而是处理问题的极高的智慧。

The doctrine of the mean is not an eclectic philosophy; it is the highest level of wisdom in solving problems.

2. 遵行中庸之道，就能避免各种极端做法，恰到好处地处理问题。

By following *the Golden Mean* we can avoid all kinds of extreme practice and deal with problems in moderate ways.

180　周而不比　比而不周

to widely unite but do not gang up
to gang up but do not widely unite
广为团结而不拉帮结派
拉帮结派而不广为团结

【出处】

子曰："君子周而不比，小人比而不周。"（论语 2.14）

The Master said, "The virtuous people widely unite but do not gang up; the virtueless people gang up but do not widely unite."

Note: Confucius pointed out the difference between the virtuous and virtueless people in handling group relationships. The virtueless people have low moral character. They are narrow-minded and often form cliques out of selfishness, and unable to get along well with the majority of people. The virtuous people are broad-minded. They act in accordance with social justice, coexist harmoniously with others, and never form cliques for personal gains.

【今译】

孔子说："君子广为团结而不拉帮结派，小人拉帮结派而不能广为团结。"

【注释】

1. 周：合群，广为团结。
2. 比：亲近，依附；（贬义）勾结，如"朋比为奸"。

【解读】

孔子指出君子和小人在处理群体关系方面的区别。小人品德低下，胸怀狭窄，往往出于私心而拉帮结派，不能与大多数人融洽相处。君子胸怀广阔。他们的行为符合社会公义，与众人和谐相处，从不为个人利益拉帮结派。

【句例】

1. 陈主任是君子周而不比，我们在他领导下工作心情舒畅。

Director Chen is a gentleman who *widely unites but does not gang up*. We are happy to work with him.

　　2. 不要把自己局限在小圈子里。我们应该从小人比而不周这句古老的格言中吸取教训。

　　Don't confine yourselves to a small circle. We should learn from this old adage: *A petty man gangs up but does not widely unite.*

参考书目　Bibliography

1. 杨伯俊今译，理雅各英译：《汉英对照文白对照四书》长沙：湖南出版社，1995 年 1 月。

2. 马恒君：《论语正宗》北京：华夏出版社 2007 年 3 月第 2 版。

3. 皇侃：《论语义疏》北京：中华书局 2013 年 10 月。

4. 杨朝明主编：《论语诠释》济南：山东出版传媒股份有限公司 2013 年 11 月。

5. 吴国珍：《论语最新英文全译全注本》福州：福建教育出版社 2015 年 11 月第 2 版。

6. 吴国珍：《论语：平解·英译》北京：北京出版社 2020 年 10 月第 4 次印刷。